Murder With a Slice of Pie

An Ivy Clark Mystery

Kristy T Dixon

For Savannah and A'lyn

Chapter 1

"Are you going to miss me?" I asked, rubbing heads with my cat. Creepers meowed, which I took as a yes. "Barbra is going to take good care of you." He jumped from my lap and walked lazily away. I brushed off my pants and climbed off the recliner.

"He's going to be fine," Barbra said from her seat on the sofa. "The two of us are going to have a blast." Barbra had agreed to stay at my house with Creepers while I participated in a baking competition. It started on a passenger train in Los Angeles and ended in Chicago.

"If you don't like staying here, you can take Creepers to your house," I said. "I know my stairs are steep." I live above my diner, and the stairway to my apartment is narrow. When the addition was added to my space, I should have had them make the stairs wider and at a more gentle slope.

"I'll be fine," she said, pushing a strand of purple hair behind her ear. "I'm in the best shape of my life."

I raised my brow.

Barbra grinned. "Okay, that might not be true. But I'm in better shape than I was when I was sixty. It must be all the Zumba you've been teaching us."

I grabbed my suitcase and made sure it was locked. "I feel bad canceling Zumba again. People are going to think I'm flaky."

Barbra tilted her head. "No one will think that. We know how busy you get, and we're just glad we get you when we do. You've checked that lock three times. Are you nervous?"

"Maybe a little. I hate to leave Creepers and the diner."

"Creepers and I will be fine, and Carrie will take good care of the diner."

"I know. Muddy Creek survived before I got here, and it will survive if I leave for a couple of weeks."

"It sounds exciting. Video cameras, judges, and a long train ride. And it doesn't hurt that you'll have the handsome sheriff with you."

I grinned. "That won't hurt at all."

"I'm glad the two of you finally realized what the rest of Kansas could see from the moment you drove into this place. It sure took the two of you long enough."

I just smiled. There was no reason to argue with Barbra. I hadn't even been here a year, so it wasn't like Jett and I had been dragging our feet.

Barbra looked thoughtful. "Being stuck on a train with Jett sounds dreamy, but you'll also be stuck with Boyd and José. That might not be as much fun and will kill any romance."

"You wouldn't want to be stuck on a train with Boyd?" I asked, grinning slyly.

"Goodness no, and don't look at me like that. Boyd is too young for me by at least five years."

"Does five years really matter once you reach a certain age?"

Barbra threw her head back and laughed. "No, I suppose not. Boyd's one of my best friends, but nothing romantic is going to happen between us. We would tear each other apart and fight all day long."

I nodded and pushed down my disappointment. I was pretty sure Boyd liked Barbra, but it must be a one-way thing.

A knock on the door made me look up.

"That must be Jett," I said, grabbing my suitcase and wheeling it to the door. I opened it to see Jett standing there wearing an enormous smile. He looked more relaxed than I'd seen him in a while.

"Ready for this?" he asked, grabbing my suitcase. He looked great in his jeans and black jacket. It wasn't often I got to see him without his sheriff's uniform.

"Have fun, Sheriff Malone." Barbra waved from the sofa.

"You too, Barbra. Don't let that crazy cat boss you around."

She laughed. "No chance. Don't let Ivy get into trouble. I know that's a lot to put on anyone."

Jett grinned. "I won't."

"I'm not planning on trouble," I said. "Call me if you need anything." I grabbed my purse, and we left.

"I can't believe how excited I am to go on an actual vacation," Jett said as we walked down the steps. "It's been a long time."

"Is this a vacation?" I asked. "I mean, it's a competition, so it might not be that fun."

We walked around from the back of the diner, and Jett put my suitcase in my gray Kia Soul. We decided to drive it to the airport instead of Jett's Cybertruck. José and Boyd were meeting us there, so we had the entire drive to talk.

"I'm off duty, out of the state, and with you. That's enough of a vacation for me." He kissed me quickly, then slammed the hatch.

We got into the car and started for the airport. The people who ran the competition were taking care of the travel expenses. We would fly to LA and board a train there.

"Had you ever heard of *The Culinary Roadshow* before José brought it up?" I asked as I drove.

"I'm not sure," Jett said, looking out the window. "It's one of those shows I would flip past without thinking about. I'm a little confused about it. How are we going to bake on the train? I watched a piece of it last night, and it didn't look like they were on a train."

"We don't. The train stops in different cities, and we do the competitions there."

"That makes more sense. And there are three teams?"

I nodded. "I can't believe we got selected. This could be good publicity for the diner."

"I'm just glad to have a reason to relax." Jett deserved a rest. He'd been working so hard as the sheriff of Muddy Creek that he never had time for himself. Things were slowly getting better now that he had three new deputies to help him and Deputy Ledford. When I first came, he was the only law in the barren county.

"I'm excited to leave the diner for a while. I love it, but it gets stale sometimes."

"I bet you'll miss your cat before we get to LA. I thought you might try to sneak him in your luggage or something."

I smiled. "Creepers hates being in the car, and I'm sure he would hate flying. I think Barbra's actually excited to stay with him."

"I hope Boyd and José are on time. I should have made them drive with us. Boyd was still eating breakfast when

I left." Boyd had recently moved in with Jett so he didn't have to live so far from town. I thought it would be a mess, but they seemed to enjoy each other's company.

"Are you worried about leaving at all?" I asked.

"No. Ledford may drive me crazy, but he's good at keeping an eye on things. All the new deputies are well-trained, so I'm sure everything will be fine."

"I should have made you drive," I said. "I've only been to Wichita when you were driving."

"You can't go the wrong way on this road. It pretty much goes straight there and nowhere else. That's one of the nice things about small towns. It's hard to get lost."

"I've been to Wichita, and it's not small."

"I'll guide you when we get into the city. Wait, doesn't your car have GPS?"

"Yes, but I don't know where to tell it to go."

Jett looked at all the buttons, then pushed one. It beeped, and he leaned forward. "Take us to the Dwight D. Eisenhower National Airport."

The car responded, "Would you like directions to this place?"

"Yes," Jett said.

"Directions will start now," said the car.

"It's crazy what cars can do these days."

"It's convenient. You can push the button on the steering wheel and talk without looking away. All cars should have that."

"I'm just glad we get to take a plane to California. I would hate to drive all that way."

⁄

I pushed a lock of blond hair behind my ear and looked out the window of the plane. We were flying over large empty fields that looked like colorful squares from up here. I hadn't been on a plane in years, and I'd forgotten how interesting it could be.

Boyd popped up from the seat in front of us and leaned against the headrest. He must have been kneeling on his seat. "The list of contestants is up on *The Culinary Road-show* website."

"Who are they?" I asked.

He looked down at his phone. "Besides Sue's Diner, the contestants are from Calico Café and The Velvet Pearl."

"What kind of place is The Velvet Pearl?" Jett asked.

Boyd scratched his bald head as his eyes ran over the text on his phone. "It's a small restaurant near a port in Florida."

José popped up next to Boyd. "It's got excellent reviews. So does Calico Café."

"Better than Sue's?" I asked.

"They're about the same. We should be evenly matched, although The Velvet Pearl has a baker who has won a bunch of awards. It looks like he lives for these types of competitions."

"I'm not worried," Jett said. "Well, if José and Ivy get sick and leave it to Boyd and me, then I'd be worried."

"You two are going to have to do some of it," José said. "It's in the rules."

"As long as you instruct us, we'll be fine."

Boyd chuckled. "You probably would have been better off taking Carrie and Anton."

José nodded in agreement. "They would have been helpful, but someone has to keep Sue's running while we're gone. Besides, I'm not sure Ivy would have agreed to come if she had to leave Creepers and Jett."

Jett grinned. "Great, I'm categorized with the cat."

"Just hope she never has to choose between the two of you," Boyd said. "I'm not sure you would win."

I smiled and shook my head. I thought these two would lay off the jokes once Jett and I officially began dating. If anything, they had gotten more annoying about them. Now, instead of teasing me when Jett wasn't around, they teased me in front of him.

"Who is the baker with all the awards?" Jett asked, lacing his fingers with mine.

Boyd looked back at his phone. "His name is Gavin Proust. He's thirty-eight and comes from Seattle, Washington. He attended the Culinary Institute of America, which is supposed to be one of the best culinary schools in the nation."

"If he was anyone to brag about, I would have heard of him," José said. "I'm sure we'll be fine."

I tilted my head as I watched him. "But if we lose, at least we get a fun trip, right?"

José shrugged. "Sure, but we're going to win."

Boyd and José turned back around in their seats.

Jett held out his phone to show it to me. "Do you want to see what the other seasons of the show were like? I only watched a few minutes last night. It might give you an idea of what we're up against."

"Will it make me nervous?"

"Hmm. Maybe. I didn't see the judges, but if you look online, it sounds like one of them can be ruthless, but only if he's having a bad day. The other one is from Italy and has absolutely no credentials when it comes to cooking. She just gives her opinion about the taste."

"I wish they didn't video it. That's the thing I'm nervous about. I don't want people watching my failures online."

"So don't fail," Jett said, grinning.

I punched him playfully on the arm. "Thanks a lot."

He chuckled and put his arm over my shoulders. "You're going to be great. You've never baked anything that wasn't delicious."

"Oh, I have. I don't give you that stuff."

"Don't stress. Even if we fail miserably, it will be fun."

I sighed and leaned against him. Failing wouldn't be the worst thing, but it wouldn't be good for the diner, either.

Chapter 2

"I can't believe I have to share a room with the three of you," I joked, pushing my suitcase into a small closet on the train. The competition had paid for each group of contestants to have a private room. Two benches in the room facing each other could be turned into beds. Two beds were hooked above the benches that could be pulled down at night.

We were all tired from the plane ride, but it was almost time for bed, so we could sleep as the train traveled across California.

Boyd sat on the blue bench and bounced up and down. "At least it's comfy. I call a bottom bed. I don't think I can get to the top bed without hurting myself."

"Me too," José said. "Let the young people take the high beds."

Jett pulled one bed down to examine it. "I thought everyone usually fought for the top bunk." He pushed it back into place.

"There comes a certain age when things change." Boyd grinned. "I bet you're getting close."

"To what?" Jett asked. "Being old?"

José chuckled. "You've still got a few years."

"I've been feeling old lately." Jett yawned.

"You should be," Boyd said. "What are you? Thirty-four?"

"Almost."

Boyd scoffed. "Double your age, and you still aren't at mine. You're still a kid."

"I had a kid call me an old guy the other day," José said. "I know I'm getting old, but I don't feel it."

"And you still have nothing on me," Boyd said. "I would love to be fifty again."

"I just hope the train ride is smooth, especially if I'm on the top bed," I said. "Falling off wouldn't be fun, and I can imagine myself doing it."

"Where's the first stop?" Jett asked, sitting next to Boyd.

"Flagstaff, Arizona," José said. "We should get there tomorrow at seven in the morning. The competition is in a culinary school."

An announcement was made over the speakers, telling everyone the train was about to leave the station.

I sat on the bench across from Jett and Boyd. "Do we know what we'll be cooking?"

José sat next to me. "We have a meeting tonight where we meet the other contestants and the judges, and they'll tell us then."

"That's not a lot of notice," Boyd said.

"No, but we have until tomorrow to do any research we might need."

I yawned. "So no going to bed?"

José grinned. "Not yet. The competitions get harder. Toward the end, we don't get to know what we're cooking until we're in the kitchen."

The train started moving, and my stomach turned. I'd never been on a train before. I was more excited than nervous.

"Once the train starts, we're supposed to go to the dining car for the meeting," José told us. "Ready?"

"I'm too old to stay up too late," Boyd said, standing.

Jett grinned. "You stay up pretty late watching movies."

"Yeah, but that's a lazy thing to do. I don't have to leave the couch."

Jett stood and held out his hand. I grabbed it, and he pulled me to my feet. José had a map of the train, so we followed him from our room and through some other cars until we got to the dining car.

The car had several booths and a wide walkway down the center. People were busy setting up cameras and lights, crowding the area. A woman about thirty, in a blazer and skirt, came over and shook my hand.

"You must be Ivy Clark," she said. "I'm Vonna Douglas, the host of *The Culinary Roadshow*."

"It's nice to meet you. This is José Garcia, Boyd Webster, and Jett Malone."

"Lovely," Vonna said, tossing her shiny black hair over her shoulder. "We are happy to have you. Your booth is over here." She led us to a table, and I scooted over by the window. Jett sat next to me, and Boyd and José sat across from us. "We'll start in a minute."

"How much of this will be recorded?" I asked.

"They record most of it but don't show as much as you would think. They only show the parts where something exciting is happening or when they're asking the contestants about themselves."

"Okay, thanks."

"We're only recording for a minute tonight, so we'll only do quick makeup and hair. Someone should come by and grab you in a second."

Vonna smiled and walked over to another table.

A woman came over and took us one by one to the car behind us and did a five-minute hair and makeup job.

Once we had all gone back, Vonna stood at the front of the car and clapped to get everyone's attention. "Hello! And welcome to the sixth season of *The Culinary Road-show*!" Everyone clapped. "We have three new groups today. Our first team is from Muddy Creek, Kansas. They are representing Sue's Diner."

The camera came close, and we all waved. I'd expected them to give us more instructions about how to act before we started.

"Next, we have a team from Tampa, Florida. They represent The Velvet Pearl."

I was happy to see the cameras move away from us and over to the table across the aisle.

"And our third team is coming to us from Calico Café in Seattle, Washington."

This was nerve-racking. I wasn't sure how well I would do with cameras and TV hosts. Vonna talked for a few minutes, but I was having trouble listening. So many things could go wrong, and all of them were running through my head.

"Tomorrow is our first round in the competition," Vonna said. I started listening again. "The contestants will make pinwheels. They can be any type. An appetizer or dessert or anything you can think of counts. Tomorrow morning, before the train pulls into Flagstaff, you will give me a list of ingredients, and they will be waiting for you when you arrive at the bake-off location. If you brought any special ingredients of your own, you are welcome to use those as well."

Panic filled my stomach. I'd never made a pinwheel before, and I wasn't sure I really knew what it was. I looked at José. He was smiling, so that helped with my nerves. He must have a recipe or at least an idea.

Vonna dismissed us all, but most people stayed in their seats to eat a quick dinner. A man from the table across from us came over. He had red hair pulled back in a ponytail and appeared to be in his mid-thirties. He wore a tight black T-shirt with a picture of a band I didn't know.

"Hello, my name is Gavin Proust. It's nice to meet the competition."

José reached out and shook his hand. "I'm José. I'm the manager of Sue's Diner." José introduced the rest of us.

Gavin studied us. "So, Kansas, huh?"

"Yep," José said.

He smiled. "There's no place like home, Toto, Dorothy, and all that?"

"I'm going to bed." Boyd stood to leave. I wanted to do the same, but I didn't want to be rude. Boyd told me once that people would excuse you for anything when you get to a certain age. He must have felt he'd reached that age.

"This competition might be a nice little thing to add to my resume," Gavin said. "I'm not an overly competitive person, but I am fantastic at baking. This show is almost too amateurish for me."

I was tired and couldn't come up with anything to say.

"Don't get me wrong," he continued, "I'm not the best there is, but I've been trained with some of the greatest bakers and chefs of all time."

"That's nice for you," José said.

Gavin held up a big turquoise bag. "I have all my secret ingredients here in my bag. I won't rely on someone else to get me certain things because they won't get the top quality. How did you choose your team? It seems a little oddly put together."

"How so?" I asked.

"None of you really look like bakers."

"What does a baker look like?" Jett asked, leaning against the seat and holding back a smile.

"Not like you. You don't bake, do you?" he asked Jett. "You look more like the bodyguard or something, and your friends all look like they host book clubs."

I frowned and looked down at my jeans and T-shirt. I would have dressed better if I'd taken the time to think it through.

Jett raised his eyebrow. "I guess you'll see what we've got tomorrow."

"Yes, I will," Gavin said. "Talk to you later. I'm looking forward to this." He turned and left the dining car.

"I'm not gonna like that guy." José ran a hand through his black hair. "Is he trying to say bakers should all look like him and be skinny, pale, and in need of a haircut?"

"Do you know what a pinwheel is?" I asked, changing the subject.

José's smile came back. "I make a mean sausage pinwheel. It looks like a cinnamon roll, but it has cheese and sausage and stuff. It's comfort food at its finest."

"I'm glad you know what you're doing because I don't think I've ever had one."

"Yep. I've got this. I'll jot down some ingredients, and we'll be good tomorrow. You might want to do a search for pinwheels just to familiarize yourself with them."

We ate quickly and went back to our small room. Jett was frowning.

"What's wrong?" I asked.

"Do I really only look like I could be the bodyguard?" he asked as he pulled down one bed.

"Ignore that guy," I said. "He's just jealous. That guy didn't have a muscle on him."

"And he smelled like tuna," Boyd said from the bench. "You can't trust the opinion of someone who smells like tuna."

I smiled. "I've seen you eat tuna."

Boyd shrugged. "Not when I have to talk to people."

Jett pulled the other bed down. "Interacting with people when I'm not on duty is weird. I don't really know how to anymore." He sat on the bench under the bed.

I sat next to him and ran my hand through his brown hair. "You interact with people just fine."

Boyd stood and grabbed his bag. "When Ivy starts messing with Jett's hair, that's my cue to leave. I'm going to get ready for bed."

"I agree," José said, grabbing his own bag. There was a small bathroom with a dressing room down the hall.

They both disappeared, and I moved onto Jett's lap. "You aren't letting that little comment get to you, right?"

He put his arms around me. "No. Things like that don't bug me. It just seemed weird. I'd take a train full of guys like that to be here with you. It's going to be great." He kissed my cheek. "I was just hoping to have most people ignore me for once while I'm here."

"That's never going to happen."

"Why not?"

I rolled my eyes. "Because you look like you and not that Gavin guy."

I wouldn't swear to it, but I think Jett's face turned a light shade of pink. I rested my head on his shoulder and pretended not to notice. Still, it was nice not to be the embarrassed one for a change.

We talked a little about the competition until Boyd came back.

"I guess I didn't stay away long enough," he said, looking at us.

I stood and stretched. "Nice pj's, Boyd. I think you might get too hot in those."

He looked down at his black-and-red-checkered flannel pajamas. "Nah. I'm always cold at night."

I grabbed my carry-on bag and went out into the hall. I almost bumped into a woman who was around fifty. "Oh, I'm sorry," I said, stepping back.

She pushed back her shoulder-length brown hair. "No problem. You're Ivy Clark, right?" A man who looked like he might be her son stood by her, looking at his phone.

"Yes."

"I'm Fiona Huxley. I'm the owner of Calico Café." She held out her hand, and I shifted my bag to shake it.

"It's nice to meet you. I didn't get a good look at the contestants. I was so nervous with the cameras."

She smiled. Her makeup was flawless, and her brown eyes sparkled. "A humble one, eh? I wish I could say I know what you mean, but I love the camera, and the camera loves me."

I was sure it did. She was really well put together. "Is this your first competition?"

"Oh goodness, no. How many is this, Keith?"

The man didn't look up from his phone. He only shrugged.

"We've been to a few," Fiona said. "This is my son, Keith."

"Hey," Keith said, not looking up.

"Hello," I said, trying not to frown. Keith looked like he was my age at least, but he reminded me of a teenager with a gaming addiction.

"Are you off to the changing room? I'll go with you," Fiona said, taking my arm and walking. Keith stood where he was, not noticing we were leaving. Fiona shook her head. "Kids these days."

"Kids?"

"I guess Keith is thirty-one. That's pretty much an adult."

I smiled. "Pretty much."

Fiona laughed. "He's my only child, so I guess I don't want to let him grow up too fast. I'm very protective. Do you have kids?"

"No."

"Married?"

"Nope."

"It's a shame young people don't get married as much as they used to. Too busy with your diner?"

"No, I just never met the right person."

"That handsome guy you were with. You two shared a few looks. Are you dating?"

"Yes."

She squeezed my arm. "Good for you. You have to watch out for the good-looking ones, though. They can be bad news. And that one you have? You better watch him close."

I held in a sigh. I wasn't sure I would get along with Fiona. Thankfully, becoming friends with the competitors wasn't part of the game. I probably wouldn't have to spend a lot of one-on-one time with them, so it wouldn't be a problem.

Chapter 3

The gentle rolling of the train lulled the others to sleep surprisingly fast, but I couldn't seem to doze off. I kept thinking that one little jerk of the train would throw me to the floor. It was after one before I fell asleep, so I was tired in the morning.

José was up and ready to go at six. I climbed groggily down from my bed and got ready. If we were on schedule, the train would arrive in Flagstaff in about an hour. I wasn't moving as fast as the others, so I was the last one to the dining car. When I got to the booth, a plate of pancakes awaited me.

"Sorry, I'm slow," I said, sitting beside Jett.

"Trouble sleeping?" José asked from across from me.

I touched my hair. "Yes. Do I look that bad?"

"You look beautiful," Jett said, putting a forkful of food in his mouth.

Boyd chuckled. "You rolled around a lot last night."

"Sorry."

"I gave the list of ingredients to the people who take care of that stuff," José stated. "Our pinwheels will be great."

"I sure hope so," I said, pouring syrup on my pancakes.

I looked around the dining car. It was packed. This must be the popular breakfast time. Fiona and Keith sat in front of us. Fiona was eating, and Keith was playing a handheld game. In the booth closest to the door was Gavin. He was talking to the people with him while waving his arms with a dramatic flair. I wondered how many people in the car were part of the competition. I wasn't sure how many people it took to run the show.

I hurried through the meal and finished just as the train stopped.

Gavin stood and walked over to Fiona, holding his turquoise bag. He said something to her, then stepped over by us.

"Good luck today," he said.

I nodded. "You too."

He winked. "I don't need luck." He walked off, whistling.

"Do we need to take our things?" I asked. "The train won't wait, will it?"

José scratched his head. "The train was booked by the competition, so everyone on it is part of the show. We leave everything we don't need here."

Fiona stood, and I gulped. She wore a cute pink pantsuit. It wasn't something I would ever wear, but I would look frumpy next to her in my tennis shoes and sweater. I hadn't planned my wardrobe well because I figured no one would see what I was wearing under my apron.

Vonna hurried down the aisle and stopped when she saw us. Her high heels clicked against the floor. She handed José a paper. "This is the address of the culinary school. Make sure you're there an hour early to get familiar with it all and have your makeup done. A car will meet you when you call the number at the top of the paper."

That meant I had time. I grew up in Arizona, and I knew Flagstaff. If I was fast, I could go get something to wear that wouldn't make me look ridiculous when I stood next to Fiona and Vonna.

A cab dropped me off in front of the culinary school. I was early, but my group had already been here for thirty minutes. They had all wanted to get here early enough not to worry about being late or at a disadvantage.

I felt a little out of my element now that I was wearing a new outfit. I tried confidently walking up to the building in my fitted black blazer and jeans. The knee-high boots I'd purchased made me five inches taller. I held four gigantic bags full of clothing and wondered what I'd been thinking.

When I got to the doors, security let me in. "There you are," the woman in charge of makeup said. I placed my bags against the wall, and she whisked me away into an unused room where three people did my hair and makeup. By the time I met my team, I felt ridiculous.

José, Boyd, and Jett stood in a room with six small kitchens. They were all leaning over a paper and murmuring.

Another kitchen had Gavin and three other men, and a third had Fiona, Keith, and their two teammates.

My boots clicked against the ceramic tiles, and everyone looked up from what they were doing. Keith even smiled when he saw me. I was such an idiot. Who cooked in high boots? I looked at Fiona's feet as I passed their kitchen. She had on pink heels, so I wasn't alone.

I avoided looking at my group as I entered our kitchen area. I didn't want to see their reactions to my new look. The area had a fridge, oven, microwave, and a few cupboards. It reminded me of my food and nutrition class in high school.

"They got you with the makeup, too?" Boyd asked. "It seems a little silly to me. They even put something on my head so it doesn't shine."

I smiled and looked at Boyd. His lips had more color than usual, and I was pretty sure someone had gotten him with concealer.

"You look nice, Ivy," José said, pulling a rolling pin out of a drawer.

"Nice?" Jett said. "You look hot." He came over and wrapped me in his arms and kissed me.

"Whoa, whoa," Boyd said. "We're in public here, and you're going to smear Ivy's lipstick."

Jett released me and grinned. "I might smear my own. I would have rethought this entire thing if I'd known about the makeup."

I took the white apron someone offered and pulled it over my head. "Is there a hairnet?"

"Nope," José said. "Vonna said that ruins the look."

"Okay, people," Vonna said, walking into the room. The cameras will be here the entire time, but only a small amount will actually be seen on the show. Look busy when they film you and answer questions I ask when the camera is on you. Feel free to talk to one another and even the other teams."

"Let's do this, people!" Gavin said. "Someday, you will all be able to say you cooked in the same room as Gavin Proust."

Vonna looked at him and raised her brow. "You still have a few minutes before we start, so if you need to run to the bathroom or anything else, now is the time."

I wasn't sure how long we would be here, so I decided to take her up on it. I hurried from the room to use the bathroom and got a drink. On my way back to the kitchens, I saw Keith squatting down by the wall near Gavin's turquoise bag. When he heard me, he stood quickly and went into the kitchen, sticking something in his jacket pocket. The bag was unzipped, but I supposed Gavin could have left it that way.

Frowning, I followed him inside. I didn't want to accuse him if he hadn't been doing anything, so I would wait and see if Gavin noticed anything missing. I went to our kitchen and walked up behind Jett. He was plugging in the mixer.

"Hey," I said quietly. He turned his head. "I think Keith stole something from Gavin's bag."

Jett groaned. "Not here, Ivs. It's a vacation, not a crime scene. Just relax."

"I'm just telling you in case Gavin says anything's missing."

"No snooping."

"I'm not. I just saw him doing something by the bag, and it's unzipped."

He nodded. "Alright, but let's not make a big deal about it unless Gavin says something."

I nodded and took a spoon José offered me.

"Two minutes until we start!" Vonna said.

"My bag!" Gavin said, running from the room. He was in and out in a flash.

"Where are the judges?" Fiona asked.

Vonna shrugged. "They don't like to mingle. They only come when they're needed."

"Were they on the train?"

"Yes, but they stick to their rooms. Let's all try to be interesting. We have a couple of networks with their eyes on us. If it's getting boring, we might need to stir some things up."

The cameras were all in position, and Vonna's smile grew as she spoke to the camera. She introduced all the teams, and I tried to pay attention.

"And our contestants think they are only making pinwheels today!" she declared. My eyes widened.

Gavin grinned. "What?"

Vonna gave a fake laugh. "Do we really need four people to make a pinwheel? Two will work on that while the other two make a dessert. It must be made with the ingredients they have or find in their kitchen!"

This might not be bad. Dessert is my specialty. If José handled the pinwheel and I did the dessert, it might go better for us.

"You may all begin!" Vonna said.

The camera came straight to our kitchen, and I tried to ignore it.

I looked at José. "I'll take the dessert."

"Have Boyd help you," José said. "If Jett does, he'll just spend all the time staring at you."

I glared at José.

"It's like that, is it?" Vonna asked, pushing a microphone in my face. "Is there some romance in the kitchen?"

Boyd chuckled. "In the kitchen, in the diner, behind the barn."

My face had to be red.

I think Vonna could tell I couldn't talk, so she moved over to Jett. "Isn't it true that you're the sheriff of Muddy Creek?"

"I am."

"And you've found love with the small-town diner owner? I guess that's why you're here?"

Jett laughed. "Something like that."

"Sounds like a warm, cozy movie."

"They sure get cozy, alright," Boyd said.

"Oh my heck, Boyd," I muttered as I looked through the cupboard. Vonna kept talking, and Boyd kept answering. I ignored it all and decided to make cheesecake. Eventually, the cameras and Vonna moved to the next kitchen.

"You're such a dork, Boyd," I said. "You too, José."

The two of them and Jett laughed.

Boyd raised his brow. "Hey, it's what the people want to hear. You don't want to be the boring group, do you?"

I took a deep breath.

"Besides, it was all true, right?"

I crossed my arms and grinned slightly. "Nothing's ever happened behind a barn."

Jett winked at me. "It can, though."

"I swear, when the three of you get together, you all get immature."

Jett squeezed my hand as he passed me. Even after dating for a month, Jett still gives me butterflies.

"Hey, does everyone know the difference between baking soda and baking powder?" Gavin asked loudly.

José rolled his eyes. "Ignore him," he muttered.

"I know," Gavin said, "but I wonder if everyone else does."

No one answered, so Gavin explained the differences while everyone else tried to block him out. It felt like he was never going to stop, but eventually, he quieted to work on his pinwheel.

Boyd helped me with the cheesecake, and we worked in mostly silence.

"No!" Gavin yelled, startling everyone. "Colby, you're such a freak!" I turned and looked over. Gavin was glaring at one of his teammates, a short man with dark hair and a goatee.

"Sorry!" Colby said. "I can fix it."

"I don't think so." Gavin grabbed a bowl from Colby's hands. "I shouldn't have trusted you with something even slightly complicated." He dumped whatever was in the bowl into the trash.

"You didn't have to throw it out," Colby complained. "It just needed a little water."

"You can't fix something by adding a little water. I'll start over. I have to do everything."

The other two men in their group shared an annoyed glance. All the other contestants tried to ignore it. Vonna was smiling and had the cameras going the entire time.

"I can't believe you are all so incompetent," Gavin said as he began chucking ingredients into the bowl. "I would kick you all off my team if I was allowed."

Chapter 4

The room was quiet. The judges had just entered and were sitting behind a table at the front of the room. On the table were six fancy serving trays. There were three pinwheels, our cheesecake, tarts, and a tray of mini carrot cakes.

"Here we are with our judges, Bianca Romano and Theo McKinley," Vonna said. She described the judges' baking histories while I studied them. Bianca was around forty, with blond hair piled up on her head in a fancy bun. She wore an elegant blue dress and looked ready for a party, not a baking competition. Theo had salt-and-pepper hair and looked about as old as José. He wore a button-up blue shirt and slacks.

"He's the actual expert," José whispered in my ear. "She's just on the show to look attractive." I nodded but didn't respond.

The judges both took bites of all the dishes and wrote things on pads of paper.

"Each dish gets a rating from one to ten points. Ten is the best," José said.

Theo pointed at the tarts. "These are excellent. It's crumbly and tender. It's almost perfect. My only complaint would be the vanilla. It's obviously imitation vanilla."

Gavin stood. "It's not imitation! I made it myself."

Theo raised his brow. "It tastes like imitation."

I leaned over to José. "How can he tell?"

José shrugged.

Gavin stomped up to the judges' table, grabbed a tart, and began chewing. "Who switched my vanilla?"

"You need to sit down," Vonna scolded, but she looked happy about the outburst.

"I won't," he muttered. "Someone tampered with my ingredients."

"If you don't go back, we'll have to ask you to leave."

Gavin growled and slunk back to his seat.

"I thought it was too tart," Bianca said with a strong Italian accent, then she laughed. "The tart was too tart."

Theo let out a breath, and Ivy would almost bet he was trying not to roll his eyes. "I give the tarts an eight out of ten."

"As do I," said Bianca.

"It should be at least a nine," Gavin mumbled.

Theo pointed at the cheesecake, and I held my breath. "The cheesecake is dense. It's creamy and rich, but it might be a tad overcooked. I give it an eight out of ten."

Bianca tapped her lip with a long blue nail. "I like it. Nine out of ten."

I took a deep breath. That wasn't too bad. Gavin was glaring at me.

"What do you think about the carrot cake?" Theo asked Bianca.

"The texture is gross, but the taste is okay. Seven out of ten."

I glanced at Fiona. She was frowning. Keith sat next to her, playing on his phone. Didn't anything get that guy's attention?

"I thought it was great," Theo said. "It was moist and spongy. And I found the texture perfect for carrot cake. Nine out of ten."

Fiona smiled.

"Now for the pinwheels," Vonna announced. "These are judged differently. Theo will rank them in first, second, and third place."

José nodded. "Good. Bianca doesn't know what she's talking about," he said under his breath.

"This one was easy to judge," Theo said. He held up Fiona's cinnamon and sugar pinwheel. "This is a cinnamon roll. I suppose you can argue it's a pinwheel, but I'm not going to buy that. It tasted fine for a cinnamon roll. He held up Gavin's ham and cheese pinwheel. Ivy frowned. It looked perfect, like something someone would take a picture of and put in a cookbook. The swirls were even and neat.

"This one was pretty good, but once again, I tasted the imitation vanilla."

Gavin jumped to his feet. "Someone traded my vanilla. This is sabotage."

"Sit down, Mr. Proust," Vonna said.

Theo held up José's sausage and cheese pinwheel. "This one was almost perfect. It looks attractive, it's tasty, and it holds together nicely. It is the clear winner, followed by the ham and cheese."

"Which one of you idiots messed with the vanilla?" Gavin glared at his teammates. "I know one of you spilled the real thing or something and didn't dare tell me. Who was it? I swear, if I find out—"

"I don't get paid enough to deal with you," one man said. He took off his apron and threw it on the floor, then left the room.

"Great! We don't need you. You're all incompetent. Anyone else want to leave?" Gavin asked his team. "I'd probably be better off alone." Another man tossed his apron and left.

"It looks like your team is down to two," Vonna pointed out.

"Good," Gavin said. "I don't need them." Colby just sat quietly in his chair.

"So the winner of this round is Sue's Diner!" Vonna said to the camera. "That doesn't mean anything, though. There are still several rounds to go! Make sure you hit subscribe in the corner of your screen so you don't miss an episode!"

"You are seriously horrible judges," Gavin said once the cameras stopped rolling.

Theo just smiled, and Bianca patted her hair.

"Even with the vanilla problem, my stuff is obviously superior. You can tell by looking at it." Vonna pointed at the cameraman, and he began filming again.

"You are overconfident, and it will be your undoing," Theo said. "Your tarts were good, but I could have made them better with my eyes shut. You're still a novice."

Gavin's face turned red, and his jaw was set. "A novice? You better watch what you say."

Theo held up his hands and looked amused. "Or what?"

Gavin stormed over to the table and leaned over it, staring into Theo's eyes. "Just watch it."

Theo stood. He was at least six foot two, and Gavin was about five foot five. Theo crossed his arms. "You wanna fight, little boy?"

Gavin stepped back and took a few deep breaths. "Sleep with one eye open." He stormed from the room. Everything was quiet, and then Theo and Vonna burst into laughter. Bianca just looked at her perfect fingernails.

"There's one every season," Theo said. "They don't usually show their colors so soon."

Vonna nodded. "He might be more intense than anyone else we've ever had. That's one reason I chose The Velvet Pearl. When I looked into Gavin Proust, I learned he had a temper."

"Gavin will be calm by tomorrow," Colby said. "You have to watch out for him when he's in a temper, but then he acts like nothing happened the next time you see him."

"So he acts like that often?" Vonna asked.

Colby shrugged. "It depends. He usually has at least one blowup like he just did every month. He even broke someone's wrist once, but he claimed he tripped and knocked them into the wall, and no one could prove anything different. Everyone who knows him knows it wasn't an accident."

"Why do you put up with him?" Fiona asked. "I wouldn't let anyone like that be on my team."

"I've learned a lot from him, and I want to be a great baker someday. A few insults won't hurt in the long run.

I'm pretty good at ignoring his outbursts. Besides, the owners of the restaurant chose who came, and Gavin is their best baker."

"Can we go now?" Fiona asked.

"Yes. We aren't going to have a big announcement tonight. The next competition is pie," said Vonna. "You all need to make two pies of the same variety. One is just for a backup. You would be amazed at how many people drop pies when they get nervous."

I frowned. I don't like pie. The last time I tried to make one, it turned out awful. José can make a great pie. They are pretty, and people enjoy them. Why couldn't we make cookies or cake? I had some great recipes for those.

"Let's do a quick interview with Boyd," Vonna said. "Sit here." She pointed at a chair set up next to an oven. "The rest of you can leave or watch quietly."

We all stood to the side, not wanting to leave Boyd.

"Tell us about yourself and why you like to cook," Vonna said.

Boyd rubbed his goatee. "My name is Boyd Webster. I grew up in Muddy Creek. My family was all farmers. I didn't want to be a farmer at first. In high school, I wrestled, and I thought about being a cage fighter when I grew up."

Jett snorted, and I covered my mouth. José just grinned and shook his head.

"My parents weren't too keen on paying for me to be a cage fighter, and I dislocated my shoulder senior year. That was the end of that dream. My mom wanted me to be a lawyer, but I don't have that disposition. I thought about running a fishing boat in Alaska, but it turns out that it's cold in Alaska, and I'm not a huge fan of the low temperatures. I elected to farm until I decided what I wanted from life, and I never figured it out, so I've been farming my entire life."

Vonna nodded. "Interesting. And when did you develop a love for baking?"

"I don't like to bake. I help Ivy out at the diner every now and then, but when it all comes down to it, I don't know the difference between baking soda and baking powder. I should have after Gavin's nice little speech, but I must have tuned him out."

Vonna asked a few more questions, then ended the interview.

"Now what?" Boyd asked. "We still have hours until bedtime." We left the kitchen area and went into the hall.

"We could catch a movie," José said.

"Sounds good."

"You guys go." I waved them off. "I think I would fall asleep if I tried to watch one."

"Do you want to walk back to the train?" Jett asked me.

"I have a bunch of bags," I said, feeling ridiculous.

"Of what?"

I sighed. "Don't tease me."

"Would I ever?"

I grinned. "Yes."

"I won't tease you."

"I might," Boyd said. "I can't make a promise when I don't know what you're going to say."

I glared playfully at him. "Thanks, Boyd. Before I moved to Muddy Creek, I was a little tight on money. It's been forever since I've gotten new clothes, and when I saw Fiona, I panicked. I didn't want to be the frumpy one."

Jett put his arm over my shoulders. "You never look frumpy."

"Well, I decided to get a few new outfits, and I got carried away."

"How carried away?"

I pointed at the four enormous bags I'd left against the wall.

Jett laughed softly. "We can send them to the train in the car, then walk."

I wrinkled my nose. "Why walk?"

"For fun?"

"You think walking is fun?"

"If it's with you."

Boyd chuckled. "You're so sappy."

I smiled at Jett. "No, he's adorable."

"That's me. Adorable." Jett grinned.

José and Boyd left, and we had my bags taken to the train. Now we were walking down the sidewalk hand in hand.

"How long will it take?" I asked.

"Probably an hour or so."

We walked quietly for a minute, but I couldn't hold it in. "I think Keith messed with Gavin's bag. What if he messed with his vanilla? Gavin doesn't strike me as the type to use imitation vanilla."

Jett sighed. "I knew you were going to bring that up."

"Shouldn't we at least check?"

"How? Snoop in his bag and taste it?"

"Maybe."

"I wouldn't know the difference. I'm not a vanilla snob."

"I might be able to tell."

"If it's really a problem, Gavin can look into it."

"But you have resources. You could get it tested or something."

Jett squeezed my hand. "I don't have any resources here. This isn't my jurisdiction. I could get in trouble for messing with things."

"Right."

"Gavin doesn't take me as a passive person. I'm sure he'll test the vanilla and do something if he really thinks something is wrong. He might have been bluffing because he was embarrassed because he used the vanilla in the first place."

"I guess that's true. Do you think Gavin will retaliate? He was mad at the judges."

"Who knows? If Colby's right, he might be over it by tomorrow."

"I guess so."

"The only contestant I'm worried about is Fiona," Jett admitted.

"Why?"

"She winked at me twice and gave me a silly little wave. I'm staying far away from her."

I laughed. "She told me you were handsome."

"Lovely. She knows she's my mom's age, right?"

"She's interesting." My phone rang, and I pulled it out. "It's a video call from Barbra." I pushed the button, and Barbra showed up on the screen. She held up Creepers.

"Creepers wants to say hello!" Barbra said. Creepers glared at the phone and meowed.

"Hi, buddy," I said. "Are you being good?"

Creepers just looked at me, then away.

"He's being an angel. We've been watching movies together. He has good taste."

I laughed. "He'll watch anything if someone holds him and pets him."

"I don't want to take up your time. I just wanted to check in."

"Thanks, Barbra."

She held up Creepers's paw and had him wave, then she hung up.

"Barbra should move to town," Jett said. "Muddy Creek has too many senior citizens who live too far from anyone. A contractor wants to build condos in town for people like that, but I don't know if he'll get the permits and stuff."

"That would be nice. I'm glad Boyd can be in town now."

"Me too. And I'm glad to have someone living with me. It makes things a lot less lonely."

"I doubt Boyd would ever let anyone feel lonely."

"Nope. It's probably good that I work a lot. He starts following me around when I get home. In a month or two, I might have to lock myself in my room to have a few minutes to think. Boyd never runs out of things to talk about."

"He needs a cat. I tell Creepers everything."

"Don't get that into his head. I'm not sure I can handle a cat."

Chapter 5

We were in a culinary school in Albuquerque, New Mexico, the following day. It was evening, and we all felt a bit of jet lag, or whatever you called it when you're on a train. Train lag? Whatever it was, we had it. The contest had already started, and we were busy making pie. Since we had to make two, José made one, and the rest of us made the other while we watched him.

"I don't think peaches and pie go together," I said as I watched José stir.

"Sure they do," Jett said. "Peach pie is amazing."

"What are you doing over here?" Gavin asked.

I turned to see him glaring at Keith. Keith stood by Gavin's kitchen with his hands in his pockets. "Nothing."

"Spying?"

"Why would I spy on you?"

Gavin's eyes narrowed. "That's what I want to know."

"I'm just bored and taking a walk around the room."

"Keith, get back here," Fiona said. "We don't need problems."

"Yeah, go back to your mommy," Gavin said as he rolled out a pie crust.

Keith took a step toward Gavin. "You enjoy being a jerk?"

I noticed Colby smile while he rolled out his own crust. Keith and Gavin glared at each other for a few moments, then Keith went back to his kitchen. He sat on a chair and pulled out his phone. Fiona glared at him. He hadn't helped a lot. Now that I thought about it, I wasn't sure if I'd seen him help at all.

The judges came in when the second pies came out of the oven. They walked around looking at the pastries and writing things on their notepads. Theo's expression didn't change. Bianca smiled when she looked at our pie, which I hoped was a good sign. She wrinkled her nose when she saw Fiona's and appeared thoughtful when she observed Gavin's.

The judges went to their table, and six pieces of pie were placed in front of them. I tried not to fidget. Yesterday, they tasted the food when we weren't watching. It was more nerve-racking like this. Theo took a bite of each pie. When he got to Gavin's, he frowned and spat it out in a napkin.

"Oh, come on!" Gavin complained.

"Your elderberries aren't ripe. I'm not swallowing that. I don't need digestive problems."

"What are you talking about?" Gavin grabbed a fork and took a big bite from the other pie.

"You aren't allowed to do that," Colby complained.

"Shut up." He took another bite, then another. "Nothing is wrong with the elderberries, but it has a strange taste."

"Perhaps that pie is better?" Bianca said. The second pie was cut and taken to them.

Theo took a small bite and spat it out again. "That was even worse. What did you put in there?"

"Let me see the first one," Gavin said, yanking the pie from an assistant's hand. He took a few bites and frowned, then took another bite from the other pie.

"You're going to make yourself sick," Theo said. "Elderberries can cause problems when they aren't ripe."

"Someone is trying to sabotage me," he said. "The second pie has an odd taste. It's not anything I put in. I bet Keith dumped something in when he was wandering around."

Keith's eyes shot daggers at him. "I didn't do anything."

Gavin took another bite of the second pie. "I taste something nutty. Someone better get to the bottom of this."

"Perhaps you should just admit your pie is bad?" Bianca suggested.

"You." Gavin pointed at Jett. "You're some kind of lawman, right? Get to the bottom of this."

"I'm a sheriff, and I have no authority here. You'll have to call the local law enforcement if you want an investigation."

Gavin dropped into a chair and glared at everyone.

"Can we move on?" Theo asked. When no one said anything, he took a bite of Fiona's strawberry pie. "It's nice. Good consistency. The flavor is powerful but not overbearing. I would sway nine out of ten."

"I like it," Bianca agreed. "It's like a burst of happiness in my mouth. I love the strawberry. Nine out of ten."

"At least she tried a little that time," José whispered.

Theo took a bite of José's pie and grimaced. "It's too salty." José frowned.

Bianca took a bite and shrugged. "Salty, but I like it."

"Really?" Theo asked. "How can you like it?"

"Don't try to tell me my opinion," Bianca said. "Seven out of ten."

"Two out of ten from me," Theo said. "I think we forgot to rate the first pie, which was also a two."

"I didn't taste it," Bianca said, taking a small taste. "One out of ten."

Gavin grumbled.

"Can I taste my pie?" José asked.

Theo nodded, and José grabbed a fork and took a bite. He frowned. "It is salty."

I went and grabbed the canister of sugar. I stuck my finger in it and put it in my mouth. It tasted like salt and sugar.

"I think someone mixed salt into the sugar," I said.

"Ha!" Gavin said. "That proves someone is trying to sabotage us, and the only group not tampered with was Calico Café."

"We didn't do anything," Fiona said. "You aren't a big enough threat to make us worry."

Gavin sneered. "We are the only threat."

Theo rubbed his chin. "I think we need to look into this. If we find a problem, this round will be redone or taken off the scores."

"It's about time someone sees reason," Gavin said. "If—" He stopped and held his stomach. "Excuse me." He rushed from the room.

"I warned him." Theo shrugged. "He'll probably be in the bathroom all night."

"He's stubborn," Colby said. "I've seen him do something similar before. A woman complained about his chicken and said it was too seasoned for anyone to be able to eat more than one bite. He sat down and ate more than a serving in front of her to prove her wrong, then ate another just for good measure. He ended up going home with a stomach ache because it *was* over seasoned."

"How do you work with him?" Boyd asked.

Colby shrugged. "Once you get used to him, you realize you can ignore him when he acts like that. He hardly fazes me anymore. It was brutal when I started working with him, but now I can tune him out."

"Well, today is a bust," Theo said. "Let's all go back to the train and get some sleep. We will put some more security around the cooking area next time."

Everyone began leaving. I opened some of our ingredients and smelled them, just to see if anything else was off. Nothing seemed odd.

Boyd laughed. "Opening a mystery, Ivy?"

I grinned. "I'm just making sure it's all normal."

"I bet they get all new stuff for the next competition," Jett said. "They don't want bad press."

"No?" Boyd asked. "Isn't bad press better than no press?"

Jett shrugged. "I guess it depends."

"We need everyone out," a security guard said. We left and took a car back to the train. I'd wanted to check the other team's ingredients, but asking would have probably made me look suspicious.

I waited patiently in line to change into my pajamas. It would have been nice to have my own room, so I didn't have to use the changing room. Fiona came up behind me.

"Crazy things today, right?" she asked.

"Yeah."

She sighed. "I'm worried about it. No one did anything to my stuff, making my team and me look guilty."

"Who are the other two members of your team? They don't talk a lot."

She waved her hand like it wasn't important. "They work at my café. They don't have anything to gain by sabotaging the other teams. I'm paying them to be here, but nothing extra."

I nodded. I didn't want to ask about Keith because that might make her angry. "It might have been a prank," I said. "A lot of people work on the staff who might have thought they were funny."

"That's true. Let's hope that's all it is. It would be stupid to sabotage everyone but myself. Only an amateur would do something like that."

It was my turn next, so I hurried and pulled on my pajamas and my pink robe. I hated walking around the train in my robe, but I wasn't going to change in my room. Maybe I could ask all the guys to leave the room for a few minutes when I got ready every day.

On my way back to our room, I saw Colby let Theo and Vonna into The Velvet Pearl's room. They closed the door, but it opened a crack. I stood against the wall and pretended to be looking at my phone.

"Where is Gavin?" Theo asked.

"I haven't seen him since the competition," Colby said.

Theo sighed. "He hasn't gotten on the train, and it leaves in thirty minutes."

"Let me call him."

I heard some things shuffle around and a minute of silence.

"It went to voicemail." Colby sighed.

"Your team is falling apart," Vonna pointed out.

"Can we hold the train?"

"No." Theo shook his head. "We have an agreement with the train station, and they have a schedule. If Gavin isn't on the train in thirty minutes, he gets left behind, and you're on your own. Are you prepared for that? Having three teams is nicer than two. I would hate to lose you."

"I'm not prepared for that at all," Colby said. "I'll do my best if it comes down to that, but I bet Gavin gets here in time."

"You better hope so," Theo said. "It won't be easy to compete by yourself against teams of four."

"He might get the underdog vote from viewers, though," Vonna said. "It might not be a bad thing."

Bianca was walking in my direction. She was wearing a silk robe, and her hair was down and shiny. She must have brushed it. I could never be as put together as Bianca because I didn't feel like brushing my hair before bed was a priority.

"Hello," I said when she passed. She didn't even look at me. I followed her since my room was in that direction, and I didn't want Theo and Vonna to see me by the door.

I pushed open the door to my room to find Jett, José, and Boyd playing a card game on the small table by the window.

"Gavin isn't on the train," I said. "No one knows where he is."

"Probably on the toilet," Boyd said. "I actually feel bad for the guy."

José looked up. "He was asking for it. A great baker should know not to eat that stuff. He was even warned. That guy needs to get a hold on his temper."

"If he isn't here on time, we're leaving him," I said. "That means Colby will be on his own."

"That will be rough," Jett said. "I wonder if he can get ahold of the other two team members and get them to return."

"I doubt it. They've already flown home. The show won't shell out money to fly them back when they left of their own accord."

"Does Gavin own The Velvet Pearl?" Jett asked.

Boyd snickered. "I bet he does. It sounds like the name he would pick."

"He doesn't," José said. "He's the manager, though."

"So it won't be a problem for Colby to continue," Jett said. "He can still represent the restaurant."

"Fiona's worried that people will suspect her of messing with people's stuff," I said.

Jett rubbed his chin. "Her team was the only one not messed with. I can see why she's worried."

"She trusts her employees."

"What about Keith?"

"I didn't ask. I figured it would only make her defensive."

"You think it was him, though. I can tell."

I tilted my head. "I didn't say that."

Jett smiled. "I can read you."

"Great, that's all I need," I teased. "I do think it might be Keith. He was messing with Gavin's bag. I don't see any reason to be in someone else's stuff unless you are up to no good."

"There are other reasons," Boyd said. "Like you're borrowing someone's toothpaste because you forgot your own."

José glared at him. "I knew someone touched my toothpaste." Boyd just shrugged, and I smiled.

Jett chuckled. "That's why I have a lock on all my bags."

"What?" Boyd gasped. "You don't trust us?"

"Nope."

"But you trust me, right?" I asked, putting my arms around Jett's waist.

He grinned and kissed my nose. "Not to snoop through my stuff? Not at all. If someone is snooping around, you would be my first guess."

My mouth turned down in a pout. "I only snoop through stuff when I'm looking for clues. I would never go through your things."

"Not unless she suspects you of a crime," José said.

I smiled. "Yeah, then I might."

Chapter 6

The following morning at breakfast, Gavin wasn't there. Even though Theo had said the train wouldn't wait, it actually had given them two hours to have the police look for Gavin. When they didn't find him, the train had no choice but to leave him behind. The police were still keeping an eye out.

This train ride would be long. We were going clear to Kansas City this time. We would do one competition on the train, taking turns using the train's kitchen. The train would have to stop a few times, but we wouldn't be getting off.

Colby sat at a table by himself. His face was propped up on his hand, and his elbow rested on the table. He was frowning and slowly stirring something in a mug. Fiona and her two employees were eating quietly.

I sat with my team and ate my eggs. They were a little soggy, but with salt, they were tolerable. Ignoring the weird squish of each bite wasn't easy.

"These eggs are gross," Jett said, putting his fork down.

José nodded. "Too much milk."

"They taste fine with ketchup," Boyd said, stabbing a ketchup-covered egg.

"That's an abomination." José shook his head. "Hot sauce, maybe, but ketchup?"

I grabbed the ketchup and put some on my eggs. "It can't make it worse." I took a bite. "It actually does taste better."

José shook his head. "I've failed with you people."

I laughed.

Keith walked into the room. He yawned and looked around the room. When his eyes fell on Colby, his eyes went wide, then he smiled and went and sat by his mom. My eyes narrowed. Something was going on with him.

"Can you guys excuse me for a minute?" I asked. I stood without waiting for an answer. If Keith was just getting to breakfast, I might have time to look in his room. I rushed down the hallway, then looked both ways before trying the door. Locked. It wasn't a good lock, though. I grabbed a credit card from my wallet and easily popped the lock. I looked both ways again and went in, closing and locking the door behind me.

The room was spotless. I wasn't surprised. Fiona always looked perfect, so why wouldn't her room? There were bags under one of the benches, but I couldn't tell whose was whose. A blue jacket hung over one chair. I recognized it as Keith's. Kneeling, I put my hand in the pocket. I quickly pulled it out because the inside was crusty. Wrinkling my nose, I wiped my hand on my jeans.

My nose wasn't sensitive, but I smelled something. I leaned closer to the jacket and sniffed. Vanilla. I tried to remember whether Keith had been wearing this jacket when I saw him near Gavin's bag. I thought he was. If he had swapped the vanilla, he might have spilled some in his jacket, which would explain the crustiness.

I heard a key in the lock. My eyes scanned the room, and I quickly rolled under the bench that didn't have bags under it. I pressed myself against the far side and held my breath as footsteps came into the room.

"This trip isn't worth it," a man said. I didn't recognize his voice, so it wasn't Keith.

"Nope," said another man. "I mean, we do get to be on a big YouTube show, but Fiona could have at least paid us more. It's so boring."

"I thought there would be more excitement. I never travel, so I thought it would be fun."

"If I'd realized there would only be cast members on board, I might have declined."

"Why does that matter?"

They sat on the bench I was under, and I could see their shoes.

He sighed. "I thought there might be some hot women to hang around when there's nothing to do."

His companion laughed. "That sounds like you. The woman from Sue's Diner is attractive."

I felt my face turn red.

"Yeah, but she's obviously with that sheriff guy in her group, and I might be vain, but I know I can't compete against him."

"Vonna and Bianca are good-looking."

"And old."

"You're too picky. They aren't that much older than you."

"Seriously? Bianca only looks good because she's had a ton of plastic surgery."

"Who cares why she looks good?"

"She wouldn't talk to either of us anyway. I heard she's got something going on with Theo, which makes sense. She has absolutely no knowledge of cooking or being a judge. Anyone can say something tastes good or bad."

"I wish someone would pay me to eat food and say my opinion."

This wasn't doing me any good. I needed to get out of here before Fiona and Keith came back. I gently pulled my phone from my back pocket and turned down the volume. I pulled up Jett's number.

I'm in Fiona's cabin, hiding under a bench. There are people in here. I need you to get them out so I can leave.

I sent the message and waited.

"Keith is driving me nuts," one man said. "He needs to get a life and stop mooching off his mom. I wish she hadn't paid his parole."

"I thought you couldn't leave the state if you were on probation?"

"He got permission."

I pursed my lips. Keith had been in prison. I wasn't surprised.

"I can't believe Fiona pays him to exist. He's put like two ingredients in while we were baking. He could at least pretend to work."

"Would you if your mom would pay you to sit around all day playing games on your phone?"

"I don't play games on my phone. Who has time for that?"

"Keith Huxley."

There was a knock on the door, and one man stood. I heard the door open.

"I think I saw a mouse go under your door," Boyd said. "You should probably go tell someone."

"Mice don't bother me," the man said.

"They bother me," the other one said, getting up. "I'll go talk to someone." I listened as his footsteps got farther away.

"Do you want to come to our room and play some cards?" José asked the remaining man. Great. José and Boyd. I wondered if Jett was there as well.

"No, thanks."

"Not a gossip, eh?" Boyd asked.

"What do you mean?"

"Everyone's talking about Gavin Proust."

"Oh yeah? What are they saying? I wasn't sad to see him go."

"Come to the dining cart, and I'll get you a dessert and tell you."

"Alright, but I'm not really hungry. I just had breakfast."

Boyd laughed. "Dessert isn't really for when you're hungry, is it?"

"I guess not." I heard the door shut, and I took three deep breaths, then rolled out from under the bench. Hurrying to the door, I peeked out. No one was there, so I walked out confidently and went to our room.

When I opened the door, I expected it to be empty, but Jett stood there with his hands on his hips.

"Hey," I said.

He raised his eyebrows. "Hey?"

I tried not to fidget. "What do you want me to say?"

"Come on, Ivs. You can't sneak into people's rooms. This is supposed to be a vacation, not a mystery."

"Don't you want to know what's happening?"

"Yes, but that doesn't mean I'm going to go into someone's room without permission."

"If I had waited for permission, we would never have solved any of our mysteries."

He took a deep breath. "I know it's pointless to argue with you, but you need to be careful."

"I'm careful."

Jett held up his phone. "I have months' worth of texts that would prove otherwise."

I wrapped my arms around his waist and smiled up at him. "And wouldn't your life be boring without me?"

He ran his hand over my hair. "Probably."

"José and Boyd had to take one of Fiona's people to the dining car for dessert. I probably owe them. It does mean they won't be back for at least ten minutes, probably more." I kissed his chin.

"I see," Jett said, arching an eyebrow. "You found a way to get rid of Boyd and José because you needed some serious kissing?"

"Maybe."

"It's because I haven't shaved for three days, isn't it?"

I smiled. "It's very possible."

"It was good of Boyd to tell me about your weird obsession with stubble."

I frowned. "Boyd never gets to know my secrets again."

He put a finger under my chin. "Well, I'm glad I was clued in." He leaned over and kissed me.

I pulled back. "Wait. I didn't tell you what I overheard."

"You can tell me in ten minutes."

Chapter 7

"I wonder why Keith was in prison," Boyd said from his seat in our room.

"Embezzlement," Jett said. "I did a search."

We were all sitting lazily on the bench with nothing to do. Even the view was boring. There was a whole lot of nothing flying by. If I looked out too long, I felt dizzy. In the morning and at night, the sky was a mixture of pink and orange, but during the day, it was weeds or grain fields as far as you could see.

"How long was he in?" José asked.

Jett looked thoughtful. "He was sentenced to three to five years. That was about three and a half years ago. I don't know how long he's been out."

A knock on the door made me jump. I got up and opened it. One of the women who did my makeup before the competitions stood there.

"Is that what you're wearing?" she asked.

I looked down at my red shirt and jeans. "Yes?"

"I think you should change."

"Why?"

"For the next round of the competition."

"When is that?"

She rolled her eyes. "It starts in an hour."

"No one told us that," Boyd said.

She smiled. "For this one, you all take turns in the kitchen. I hope you are all good at working with each other so you can figure out what your team is thinking when they aren't with you."

I frowned. I had no idea what she was talking about. "I can grab some different clothes."

"Yeah, do that."

I grabbed one of my bags and pulled out a red dress I bought in Flagstaff. It wasn't something I would normally wear, but when I tried it on, it looked so good that I'd gotten it. Now, I was self-conscious about wearing it. People staring at me made me feel funny, so I tried to avoid it. I grabbed the strappy red shoes I'd gotten to match and followed the woman.

Once my hair and makeup were done, I looked like I was on my way to a party, not the kitchen. I pushed a blond curl behind my ear and followed a woman to the kitchen, where I met Vonna.

"Hello," she said. I tried to ignore the cameras. "Today is a surprise competition. You will make a cake with no recipe. It needs to have two layers. You won't make the frosting or anything besides the actual cake. Your teammates will do the other parts."

I could make a cake, no problem. I wondered what strange things Jett and Boyd would do when it was their turn. They could cook if given instructions, but if they had to improvise, anything could happen.

Vonna wanted to do my interview while I got ready. While I gathered the ingredients, she asked me questions about solving crimes in Muddy Creek. I wondered if my history of solving murders was why Sue's Diner was selected.

Baking in high heels was ridiculous. At least I knew Fiona would be dressed to the nines as well. Of course, I wouldn't see her if we were all taking turns.

I answered Vonna's questions, but probably not the way she wanted. Details of some crimes I'd solved didn't need to be broadcast across the internet. It was also hard to come up with a cake recipe while someone asked questions. I began tuning her out and focused on the cake. Eventually, she stopped talking.

Chocolate cake might seem like an easy out, but if you get too experimental with cake, you risk making something fancy that tastes bad. I go with taste over appearance every time. Someone might forgive an ugly cake, but they won't forget something nasty. I grabbed the cocoa powder and began measuring.

By the time the cake was out of the oven, I was ready to run. Vonna had asked as many questions as she could while it baked, and I was exhausted.

"I'll stop with the questions if you just give a quick outline of your life since you came to Kansas," she said. "Start over and pretend we've never done an interview."

I sat in the chair and tried to smile. "My name is Ivy Clark, and I own Sue's Diner in Muddy Creek, Kansas. The diner was started by Sue, my grandmother on my mom's side. I live above the diner with my cat, Cosmic Creepers."

"Cosmic Creepers?" Vonna asked. "Like from *Bedknobs and Broomsticks*?"

"Yes."

"When did you find a love for baking?" she asked.

"I used to bake with my mom when I was young. I've always enjoyed it."

"Can you say something interesting or slightly controversial?" Vonna prodded.

"Sorry. I'm boring."

"You've solved more than one murder in your small town. Nothing about that is boring."

"I'm not going to talk about those things, but I do enjoy solving mysteries."

Vonna let me go once she realized I wasn't going to say anything exciting.

I went back to my room and entered. José was gone. He must be getting hair and makeup done. That meant he would be making the filling for the cake that would go between the two layers. Probably a good idea. That would leave frosting and decorating for Jett and Boyd.

I blinked a couple of times, bringing myself back to the present and out of my thoughts. Jett and Boyd were both staring at me. Jett's mouth was hanging slightly open. I wondered if I'd missed something.

My eyes widened. "What?"

"Hey, Boyd, go away," Jett said.

Boyd chuckled. "Yep." He stood and left the room.

I frowned. "What's going on? Why did you send Boyd away?"

Jett stood and looked sheepish. "You should wear that dress every day."

I felt my face match the color of the dress. "I probably shouldn't have gotten it."

"Oh no. You totally should have." He walked over and grabbed my hands. "You look so good. I don't even have the right words. Don't get me wrong, you always look good, but this dress is perfect." He put his hands around my waist and kissed me. I sighed. Maybe I was glad I had the dress.

The train began to slow, and we pulled apart. Jett looked out the window. "We shouldn't be slowing down. We aren't anywhere near a station." He frowned and moved closer to the window, pressing his face against it. "Two motorcycles are catching up to us."

I leaned against the window to see. "Why would the train stop for them?"

Jett shrugged. "They could be some type of law."

"On motorcycles?"

"It would probably be the best way to get here. There aren't any roads around." The train stopped, and Jett chewed on the inside of his cheek. "I'm going to go talk to them."

"But you said you don't have any jurisdiction."

"I don't, but I can still give them some information." He kissed me quickly and disappeared through the door.

A few minutes later, Boyd came back. "Some FBI agents boarded the train. They asked everyone to clear the halls. Where's Jett?"

"He went to talk to them."

"Well, I guess we wait here and play UNO?"

"Sure," I said, going over to the table. We played a few rounds, then Jett came in.

"What did they want?" Boyd asked.

"The police in Albuquerque found Gavin's body," Jett said.

My eyes went wide. "What?"

"He was in a gas station bathroom. The FBI took over since they assume the killer is on the train."

"They think he was killed?" I asked. "It wasn't from the weird berries?"

He sat next to me. "I don't know. They think whatever happened is related to the competition. They weren't saying a lot. I'm sure they'll question everyone."

"Did you tell them about Keith?"

"Not yet. They only talked to me for a minute. I have a feeling they aren't the type to want anyone to help them with their jobs." He looked at me.

"Are you telling me to stay out of it?"

He grinned. "Nope. I know better. I'm just warning you. If you poke your nose into this, you might get in trouble."

"Why do you suppose Keith would go after Gavin? I mean, I know Gavin thought he was a big deal, but José is good as well." I was already ignoring Jett's warning.

"You don't know it was Keith," Jett said.

"Yeah, but it's my guess at the moment."

"Someone sabotaged our sugar," Boyd reminded me. "Maybe they didn't mean to kill Gavin. It might have seemed like a harmless thing that went wrong."

"True." I tapped my lip. "What if they weren't targeting Gavin? The contestants don't usually eat the food. They might have been after one or both of the judges."

"That's a really big possibility," Jett said. "Although we don't know that the pie killed him. The toxicology report isn't in yet."

Someone knocked and pushed open the door. "We're ready for Boyd," said the makeup woman. I really should learn her name.

Boyd sighed. "I never thought I would be going in for hair and makeup."

Jett grinned. "Especially not hair."

Boyd laughed and rubbed his bald head. "They do something to my goatee that makes it soft." He left with the woman, and I turned back to Jett.

"I need to stop thinking it's Keith. It's possible he just bent down by Gavin's bag, and I jumped to a conclusion. For all we know, it's Colby, and he wanted Gavin out of the way so he could get the recognition."

"That's possible. Or it could be Theo who didn't like the way Gavin talked to him after the first round. Or Bianca, who is secretly dating Theo, but everyone knows. It could be anyone on the crew. It sounds like Gavin was rude to the woman who did his makeup, so he's probably been rude to just about everyone."

"I don't know most of the crew. Especially all the technical people." A lot of people were involved in the competition. Most were behind-the-scenes people and didn't have a lot to do with us. My money was still on Keith, but I couldn't have a narrow mind.

"The agents will figure it out," Jett said. "I'm not too worried."

"How long will the train be stopped?"

"I don't know. It could be a while if they want to talk to everyone."

I leaned against my seat. "I'm surprised they sent the FBI and not the police."

"The FBI doesn't have to worry about things like state lines and jurisdiction. If the train starts up again, they could stay on if they needed to."

"Do we know when they'll talk to us?"

"No. We just need to be ready. You might want to change."

"Into what?" I'd never talked to FBI agents before. I wasn't sure what would be expected.

Jett grinned. "Something less...wow. Maybe an old bathrobe? And you could put curlers in your hair or something. Those agents aren't old, and they aren't ugly."

I tilted my head and smiled at him. "Are you worried I'll fall for a random FBI agent?"

Jett scooted closer to me on the bench and put his arm around me. "Nah, I'm not the jealous type."

I raised my brow. "Oh no? What about poor Brian? All he did was mind his business and be polite while he ran the library, and you were always giving him the worst glares."

"Okay, okay, but in my defense, that was before we were dating, and I didn't know what you were thinking."

The door opened, and José came in. "Our cake is looking great," he said. "Too bad Boyd and Jett will probably ruin it."

"Hey!" Jett said. "Are you saying you don't have any faith in us?"

José grinned and stretched his back. "You're a great sheriff. I'm just saying don't quit your day job to become a chef or anything. I'm guessing they will have Boyd do the frosting and you do something on top," José said. "Boyd's helped at the diner enough that I think he'll be able to handle a simple frosting. I did a chocolate mousse for the center, so that should overpower a frosting that isn't high quality. At least I hope."

"Any advice for me?" Jett asked.

"Just don't get too creative. Think about eating it. If you wouldn't want to eat it, don't put it on."

"I can handle that."

"Why did the train stop? Someone said something about the FBI?"

"Yeah, they found Gavin's body. They're questioning everyone."

José whistled. "Well, dang. Do you ever wonder if we are bad luck? These things seem to find us."

"No, it's just weird," I said. "Really weird. Of course, we jump into these things once they happen."

Jett smirked. "Do we?"

"Well, you usually have to since it's your job, and I jump in and drag José and Boyd with me."

"And occasionally Brian."

I smiled. "Brian's safe this time."

Chapter 8

We sat in the dining car, and the judges stood at the front of the car with three cakes on a small portable table. The two FBI agents had asked to be present so they could observe. They sat in a back booth away from the cameras and the people running around with microphones.

Theo held up Colby's cake. It was white with fancy piping. When Theo cut a piece, it was white cake with something red in the middle. The judges both took a bite.

"It's pretty. The flavor is good, but it's dry," Theo said. "I like the strawberry filling. Eight out of ten."

Bianca sighed. "It's boring. The strawberry is too sour. Seven out of ten."

Colby nodded and sagged back against his seat.

Theo held up our cake. It wasn't beautiful, but it was alright. Boyd's frosting was a bit messy.

"What's on top?" I whispered to Jett.

"Crushed-up pretzels."

"What else?"

He shrugged. "That's all."

"In all the time you were in there, all you did was crush up pretzels?"

"Yep."

I pressed my hands together nervously.

"I figured the more I did, the worse it would be. I thought about cutting up gummy bears and putting those on top, but I changed my mind."

I was glad he hadn't done that.

"It's messy," Theo said.

"Very unattractive," Bianca agreed.

They both took a bite, and I watched José's leg jiggle nervously up and down.

"The flavors are good together," Theo said. "The mousse is light and airy, and the cake is moist. The pretzels add a nice crunch. I give it a nine."

Bianca nodded. "Wonderful. Nine from me as well."

Fiona's cake looked like a professional cake decorator had made it. Both of the judges gave hers a nine. Vonna recapped the scores for the camera, and I was glad I hadn't changed out of my red dress. Vonna, Bianca, and Fiona all looked perfect.

After the round, the cameraman found everyone again and tried to get us to say interesting things about ourselves. Vonna told us it was better if we had something emotional to say, and if we could cry, that helped get the audience to connect. I probably irritated them because I never gave them much. I don't cry on cue, and I don't want to cry on camera.

Boyd loved those moments. He would go off on all sorts of stories about his life. Jett and José would be in the background trying not to laugh. I wondered if half of the stories were even based on something real, or if Boyd just made it up to make Vonna happy. I'd hoped they would skip that part today since the FBI was here, but they came as soon as we got to our room.

The rooms on the train were small, and having this many people, plus a camera, was cramped. I volunteered to go first so I could leave the cramped area as soon as possible.

Vonna stood to the side of the camera. "Is there anyone you miss back home?"

"I brought most of my close friends with me," I said lamely.

"No beau?"

Boyd snickered, and I glared at him. Thankfully, most of what they recorded would get cut out.

"I brought him as well," I said. Vonna already knew this. She even mentioned it on camera on the first day.

Vonna's eyes went wide with fake shock, and she looked behind her at the rest of my team. "How did I miss this? The sheriff, I'm guessing?"

"Yep." I felt ridiculous. Jett winked and nodded at me. He knew I was nervous.

"Let's get Jett over here with you." Vonna grabbed Jett's arm from where he sat on the bench behind and pulled him around the cameraman. "Put your arm over her." Jett did as he was told. "Now, one of you tell your story. Or both of you, one at a time, and we'll turn it into something great. Jett, you start."

Jett blew out his breath. "Well, Ivy came to Muddy Creek last year. She took over her grandma's diner." He turned and smiled at me. "I still remember the first moment I saw her. I remember thinking she was definitely going to make Muddy Creek more interesting. Muddy Creek is small, so I walk around the square several times a day to make sure everything is safe. Once Ivy came, I started stopping by the diner on my route each day."

I felt my stomach flutter. I didn't know if he was making it up for Vonna. He had come into the diner almost every day when I started. I thought that must be normal. Jett talked for a while longer, and then one of the FBI agents poked their head into the room.

"We need to talk to Ivy Clark now," he said. I stood and hurried out. With luck, I wouldn't have to go back to this awkward video session. I was glad I got to hear what Jett had to say, but I was nervous about what I would reveal. My parents didn't even know I was dating anyone. I hated to tell them and have them disappointed if it didn't work out. I was almost sure Jett was the one, but I was still being cautious. I would have to tell my parents before the show aired.

I followed him to an empty room, and his partner joined us. "Please sit," he said, pointing at the bench. I sat, and they sat across from me. He ran a hand over his short black curls. "I'm Agent Levi Archer, and this is Agent Evan Blake."

"Nice to meet you," I said, trying not to feel nervous. I hadn't done anything.

"You probably know we're here to investigate the murder of Gavin Proust."

I nodded.

Agent Archer rested his elbows on his knees and leaned forward, his deep brown eyes on me. "What was your relationship with Gavin Proust?"

"I only talked to him once or twice and only for a minute."

"Your diner was competing against his, correct?"

"Yes."

"Was he a threat to you?"

I shrugged. "Not to me, personally."

"But to the competition?"

"Sure. Everyone in the contest is a threat, if you mean they might win."

"How important is winning the contest to you?"

"It would be nice for publicity, but honestly, win or lose, I'll be fine."

"What made you enter the contest?"

"My manager entered. I didn't even know about it until we were accepted."

"And that would be José Garcia? Not the actor?" He smiled.

My brows came together. "Actor?"

"There's an actor named José Garcia."

"Oh," I said lamely.

"Do you think anyone on your team would tamper with another team's baking?"

"No. I know them all really well."

"Did you tamper with anything?"

"No."

The other agent leaned back against the wall and looked bored. His sandy-blond hair was a bit messy. Probably from coming in on a motorcycle.

"We spoke with Sheriff Malone. He said you had some suspicions. Can you share them with us?"

"I don't want to point a finger without any evidence."

"We won't accuse someone just because you suspect something, but we'll look into it."

I wasn't sure why I was so nervous. "Before one round of the contest, I saw Keith Huxley messing around with Gavin's bag."

"You're sure it was Gavin's bag?"

"It's turquoise, so it stands out."

"Do you think Keith was sabotaging it?"

"I don't know if he was, but I suspect he was." I wished Agent Archer would blink. He had excellent eye contact.

"Is there any reason you believe that besides him touching the bag?"

"I overheard he was on probation. Not that it makes him guilty."

The two men shared a look, and I was finally able to blink hard.

Agent Archer looked back. "We know you have a history of solving crimes. Please don't try that here. We have it under control."

I crossed my arms, and my mouth turned down. "Did Jett tell you that?"

"Jett?" he asked.

"Sheriff Malone."

"No, that must have slipped his mind. We gathered information about everyone on the train." He turned to his partner. "The sheriff should have mentioned it if he knew. Go get him."

Agent Blake opened the door and looked down the hallway. "He's just down there. Hey, Sheriff!" He motioned him over with his hand.

"He was part of everything I solved. Shouldn't that have been in the information you gathered? In fact, my entire team all helped."

Agent Archer smiled. "So you cook all day and solve crimes at night?"

"Something like that."

"Well, stay out of this one. We've got it."

"You're wasting your breath," Jett said when he entered. He sat next to me. "If you want to keep Ivy out of it, you'll have to lock her up or throw her off the train. Believe me, I know."

I scowled at him, but he was right.

Agent Archer chuckled. "Is that why you let her do things she shouldn't? Because you would have to kick her out of town?"

"That, and I figure it's safer if I know what she's up to."

My eyes narrowed. "I hardly ever do things that aren't safe."

"Digging up a grave in the middle of the night?"

"How is that dangerous? The guy was dead."

Both agents burst into laughter. I couldn't believe Jett was ratting me out.

"How about chasing a suspected murderer into a corn maze?"

I rolled my eyes. "I didn't say I never do anything dangerous, just hardly ever."

"Well, we don't want you getting into trouble here, alright?" Agent Archer said. "You leave it all to us, and we won't tie you up or toss you from the train. Deal?"

I pursed my lips and tried to think of a way to look like I was agreeing without actually agreeing.

"That's the look she gets when—oof." Jett was cut off by my elbow in his side. "Come on, Ivs. It's better they know what they're getting into. Don't give me that look." I wasn't sure what look I was giving him, but I was pretty sure he deserved it.

"I'll try not to do anything besides watch and listen, but I'm not making promises." I gave Jett one more dirty look, and he shrugged.

"Are you two dating?" Agent Archer asked.

"We were until one minute ago." I didn't mean it, but I was embarrassed.

Jett blew out a long breath.

Agent Archer gave him a sympathetic smile. "I'll let you two go. If I need anything else, I'll find you."

I stood and stormed out. I went to our room and closed the door behind me. I didn't even slam it like I wanted to. The door began to open, and I pushed it shut and leaned on it. Jett pressed on it, gently sliding me back, thanks to my ridiculous shoes. He came in and closed the door. I crossed my arms and glared at him.

"I'm sorry, Ivs. I thought they needed to know. It's better for them to be prepared in case they go into a room and find you somewhere you aren't supposed to be. They won't think you're up to no good."

"That was so embarrassing. You made me sound like a little kid who can't obey the rules."

He raised his brow as he looked at me.

"I know. I am like a kid who doesn't obey the rules," I mumbled. "It sounds bad when you talk about it, though."

Jett pulled me into his arms, and I buried my face against his chest. "It drives me crazy when you put yourself in danger to solve a crime. It's also one of the things that draws me to you. You're strong and smart. You've saved me more than once. I'm sorry I embarrassed you. We tease each other all the time, and you don't seem to mind."

"Not when it's in front of friends."

"So it's not cool in front of the hot FBI agents?"

I looked up at him and frowned, then smiled. "They are hot, aren't they?"

He frowned. "You could at least pretend to disagree."

"Don't worry. They have nothing on you."

"And we're still dating? And you're still madly in love with me?"

"I am. Even though you're a punk sometimes."

He grinned. "I can live with that."

Chapter 9

The train was still sitting on the tracks the following morning. I had another video call with my cat, then I tried to read a book. Leaving things to the FBI shouldn't be hard. I knew they were qualified, but something in me couldn't leave things like this alone.

Bianca and Theo were running around with the camera people, trying not to waste time. They had already talked to me today. I hadn't seen Vonna. She was usually the one doing that type of thing.

Jett kept pacing up and down the train aisles. I knew he said he was staying out of things, but I think it was hard for him to stand back completely. He was used to keeping busy and didn't know what to do with idle time.

José and Boyd were playing UNO again. They had played so many times it should have made them crazy.

They never ran out of things to discuss, so they kept playing and talking. I played a couple of rounds, but that was all I could take.

I wandered out into the aisle, hoping to spot Jett. Vonna was walking with her back to me. When she passed Fiona and Keith's door, she knocked two times and kept walking. My mouth turned down. She swiftly disappeared from my view. A moment later, Keith came out of his room and went in the same direction.

No way was I letting this go. I followed a short distance behind him. He went out of our car and into the next. I paused for a few seconds, then opened the door. Keith was already moving to the next car. This one was full of empty seats. It made sense since the people on the show were the only ones on the train, and we weren't moving.

When Keith came to the last door, he opened it and exited the train. That was just great. With my luck, I'd follow him out and get left behind. I looked out the small window on the back door and saw Keith and Vonna standing on the platform. They were leaning against a small railing and looking forward.

I ducked down and touched the door handle. Someone put their hand on my shoulder. I spun around to see Jett. He put a finger to his lips. He crouched and slowly opened the door a few inches and moved to the side. I squatted on the other side.

"You got too carried away," Vonna said. "Why can't you just follow instructions?"

"I don't know what you're talking about," Keith said. "I did exactly what you told me."

"No, you didn't. I am not going down with you."

"Don't worry about that. It was all a mistake. Baking accidents can happen to anyone, and Gavin was an idiot. It's not surprising he was taken out by his own cooking."

"Is that what the police will find?"

"I don't know why you're being like this," Keith said. "Who's to say you didn't do something? You're the one who wants the ratings so badly."

"You know that's ridiculous."

"Do I? You know no big station is going to pick up the show. Even I can tell it's not professional, and it's boring."

"It's not boring, and we don't have the funds to be better than we are."

"Well, you're getting attention now. I don't see why you're upset. Gavin failed. He failed badly enough to be dead. Maybe that means he deserved it. He was the one bragging about how great he was. Obviously, he didn't know what he was doing."

"I guess," Vonna said.

"There's no reason to get bent out of shape about this, alright? You're freaking out about things that you shouldn't."

It was quiet for almost a full minute, or at least that was how it felt. I tried to look through the small crack in the door, but it was hard to see anything. Standing slowly, I peeked out the window and grimaced. They were kissing. The fancy and talented Vonna Douglas was kissing the phone addict and much younger Keith Huxley.

I motioned with my head to tell Jett we should leave, and we quietly left the train car.

"They were kissing!" I said as we walked through an empty car. "That is so wrong."

"Why?" Jett asked.

"She's obviously manipulating him or something. Vonna must have convinced Keith to do something to make the contest more exciting, and he got carried away."

"That's what it sounded like, but no one actually confessed. Vonna seems to think Keith did something, but he didn't admit to anything."

"Next time we go on vacation, let's make sure it's a real vacation."

Jett took my hand. "There will be a next vacation?"

I just shrugged. I sure hoped so. "Should we tell the agents?"

"About our next vacation?"

I bumped my shoulder into him. "You aren't as funny as you think you are."

"I'm not sure. If we tell them, they might get annoyed that we were following Keith. Well, you were following him. I was following you."

"I can tell them and keep you out of it. Just so you don't get in trouble."

"That's when things get suspicious. Once you start telling half-truths to law officers, you lose credibility."

"Okay, so we tell them the entire truth. I followed them, and you followed me, then we went back to our room to play the hundredth game of UNO."

"We should have brought more games."

We stopped in front of the room, and I looked at the time on my phone. The dining car served dessert almost all day. "I'll go get some dessert and bring it back."

Jett nodded and went inside.

I hurried to the dining cart and ordered four brownies and sat at a table while I waited. It was possible to have things delivered, but I didn't want to pay the fee. Colby was sitting at a table by himself. When he saw me, he picked up his papers and came to my table.

"Any word on how much longer we'll be sitting here?" he asked me.

"Not that I've heard."

"I don't get why we have to stop. I'm ready to be done with this entire thing."

"Oh yeah?"

He ran a hand over his face. "I would leave, but I still have my job to consider. I'm representing The Velvet Pearl, and the owners are counting on me. They're really stressed about Gavin and about the other two leaving. I bet they got fired."

"I'm sorry. It would be hard to do the contest alone."

"I'm not the best at The Velvet Pearl. I'm not terrible, but I'm nowhere near as good as Gavin was. He would make something from any ingredients. I'm good at following a recipe but not being creative."

"I know what you mean. I prefer a recipe to doing my own thing. José is great at making things up in his head, but that's not my talent. I'm sorry you lost a coworker."

Colby ran his finger over his goatee. "It's sad, but honestly, we weren't close. I'm upset it happened. He was my mentor, after all, but as a person, he sucked. No one in the restaurant liked him. He thought he was so much more talented than anyone else, and he said it often. That's not a good way to make friends. It's good he didn't die back home. Everyone would have had a motive."

"You don't seem worried about becoming a suspect."

"Nah. I had no reason to get rid of him. I'm pretty sure it was Keith. He was over by our stuff a lot. He was usually looking down at his phone, but why come stand by our ingredients to play a phone game? It just happened too much to be normal."

"Did you tell the agents?"

"Of course."

"How do you think he died?" I asked. "From the elder-berries?"

He rubbed his goatee again. "Do you know much about elderberries?"

"No."

"I didn't either until Gavin died. I searched for them on-line. If they aren't ripe, they can cause all sorts of problems. Cramps and digestion issues, even death."

"How could that be blamed on Keith?"

Colby shrugged. "Gavin insisted on purchasing all our ingredients. He wouldn't let the people here get them because he thought they wouldn't get quality things. There's no way Gavin would get unripe berries."

"So you're saying someone switched out the berries?"

"That's my guess. And dumped the crushed cashew shells in. They might have been what really killed him."

My brows came together. "Cashew shells?"

"Yeah, someone ground them up and got them into our pie somehow."

"Wouldn't that show on the video?"

"Not if they mixed them in with some of the other ingredients."

I tapped my fingers against the table. "What's wrong with cashew shells?"

"The shells have a chemical called urushiol. It's toxic. That's why they roast cashews to make them safer to eat."

"How do they know they were in there? Did the toxicology report finally come in?"

He looked confused and shrugged. "Maybe they tested the actual pie?"

I nodded. "Do you think they were targeting Gavin or the judges? Gavin wasn't supposed to eat it."

"That's true. Who would want to hurt the judges? I mean, Gavin was really mad at them, but it would be dumb of him to poison the pie, then eat it himself."

"It could be anyone. It might not even be related to the contest."

"That's something to think about. Do you think the agents know it might have been aimed at the judges?"

I shrugged. "Probably. It makes sense. It's against the rules for contestants to eat their creations until after everything is filmed, so no one should have suspected he would."

"I think I'll go mention it to them, just in case they hadn't thought of it." He stood and grabbed his things. "I'll talk to you later."

"Bye." I waited a few more minutes for the brownies, then took them to our room. Jett, José, and Boyd were at the table playing a matching game with the UNO cards.

"Yes! Sustenance," Boyd said when I handed him a brownie.

I handed them to the others and smiled. "Sustenance, eh?"

Boyd smiled as he took a big bite.

"I hope we get moving soon," José said. "We don't want to be away from the diner longer than we have to."

"Did you guys hear that Gavin's pie had ground-up cashew shells in it?" I asked.

"Really?" José said. "That didn't happen by accident."

"Why would they use those?" Jett asked.

"They're poisonous," José said. "That, plus the unripe elderberries, must have made for a painful time until he died. I'm surprised they could hide that in a pie. They must have ground it up pretty well to make it go unnoticed. I've never eaten it, but I would think it would taste bad."

"I think it did," I said. "Everyone who tasted it said it was gross."

"I thought we would see more of the FBI agents," Boyd said. "They only talked to me for a minute."

"They have a lot of people to question," Jett pointed out. "The crew for the show isn't as big as some, but it's big enough. I bet they have somewhere around fifty people."

"How did you find out about the cashews?" José asked.

"Colby just told me. He was in the dining car," I said.

"That poor guy." José shook his head. "It would be rough to have to do the work of four people. It's too bad the rest of his crew quit."

"He's determined to keep going. His job seems to be important to him, so he doesn't want to let people down."

"This entire thing is turning into a mess for him," José said. "I'm actually surprised the judges are letting him compete alone."

"Vonna did say something about him getting the sympathy vote from the audience. I don't think they care that it's hard for him. I think they like that it's giving them publicity."

"The show should probably have all the ingredients locked up and not let anyone near them," Jett said. "If there's another season, I bet they have a lot more restrictions. I doubt anyone will be allowed to bring any of their own ingredients."

Boyd took a bite of his brownie. "Let's just hope the train gets going again. We don't want to stay here until we run out of desserts or anything."

Chapter 10

I rolled over on my bed and opened my eyes. Someone stared at me in the dark. I let out a muffled scream as a hand covered my mouth.

"It's Jett," he said quickly.

My heart was beating out of control. "What are you doing?" I demanded in a loud whisper. "You almost gave me a heart attack!"

"I had a dream that you were chasing someone on the top of the train while it was moving. I had to get up and make sure you were still here. I didn't mean to wake you."

"Do you really think I would chase someone on a moving train?"

"If you thought you might catch them, then yes."

"Don't worry. I'm not planning on it."

"Sorry I woke you."

"It's alright. You're lucky I didn't hit you or anything. You look creepy in the dark."

"What's going on?" Boyd asked from the bed underneath me.

"Jett's just having weird dreams," I said.

"Hmm. Okay."

"Jett, get back to your bed," José muttered. "It's after midnight."

"I'm going," Jett said, turning and climbing back on his bed. "That was a freaky dream. Everyone make sure Ivy stays off the top of the train."

"I'm not getting up there," I said. "You've seen too many movies."

"You will if you're after someone, and they go up there," Boyd said.

I rolled over and pulled my blanket up to my chin. He was probably right. Once I had my mind set on something, it was hard not to follow through. Still, the top of a moving train was a scary thing, and I might have enough sense not to climb up there.

"Now I'm gonna have to get back to sleep," Boyd complained.

"You wake me up at least five times a night with your snoring," Jett said.

I smiled. All of them had woken me with snoring, but Boyd was definitely the worst. I'd woken in a panic a few times because of it. After my heart settled, I didn't have a hard time falling back asleep.

The following morning, it was raining, and the train still wasn't going anywhere. I was surprised no other trains seemed to need these tracks. Maybe because we were in the middle of nowhere. I wasn't even sure what state we were in. It was either New Mexico, Colorado, or Kansas. I knew our next destination was Kansas City, but I didn't know where we stopped. If I remembered the map right, we were only cutting the corner of Colorado.

"Hey, everyone," Boyd said, sitting next to José at the booth in the dining car. Jett and I sat across from them. We'd already finished eating, but we didn't have anywhere to go. "The train is going to start soon."

"Did the FBI finish their investigation?" I asked.

"No. They're going to stay on, and the train will move slowly. Trains have been taking a small detour around us, but a train coming through tomorrow has to come on this track. If we move slowly, we can make it to a station where we can stop before they need to pass us. They were just loading the agents' motorcycles into one of the empty cars."

"I'll be glad to be moving again," Jett said.

"Oh," Boyd said. "I also saw someone with a hoodie pulled up over their head walking down the aisle two cars back. Why wear a hood inside? It looked suspicious to me, but I got distracted and forgot until right now."

"I'll be back," I said, standing.

Jett groaned. "Come on, Ivs. Anyone could be wearing a hood. It's cool today. He pointed at the overcast sky out the window.

"I'm not doing anything crazy," I said, climbing over him to the aisle. "I'll be right back."

I hurried through the train cars, and when I got near the back, I saw someone walking with their back to me in a black hoodie. I waited patiently for them to go to the last car. After giving them a minute, I cracked the door. The person had the caboose door open and was throwing something. I closed the door and moved over behind some stored luggage.

The door opened, and I watched the person hurry past. I couldn't make out who they were. Staying hidden was difficult, but I waited an entire minute before going out the back door. I went down the three steps and jumped from the train. I scanned the ground around me and found a sandwich baggie. It was almost empty, except for a bit of dust inside. I opened it and smelled it. There was a musty smell, but nothing I could identify.

I looked around to see if there was anything else, but this was it. The train made a noise behind me, but I was too busy thinking to process it. When the train began moving, my brain finally kicked in, and I rushed and jumped on the step, then grabbed the railing. I got onto the small platform and watched as we slowly left the area. The bag was now safely in my pocket.

I turned and pulled on the handle, but it was locked. I frowned. It wasn't the worst thing. Jett knew I was looking for someone and wouldn't wait long before coming after me. My phone was still on the table in the dining car. A slight chill went up my spine when it dawned on me that the door hadn't been locked when I went out. Perhaps one of the train workers had locked it, or maybe it only opened from the inside.

Turning, I leaned against the rail and watched the miles of weeds pass behind us. The door opened, bumping me to the side. Expecting Jett to pop into view, I pushed the door, but met with resistance. The door moved slightly, then slammed into me. Whoever it was, wasn't a friend. I took a deep breath and plowed into the door as hard as I could. I expected the person on the other side to be stronger, but after struggling for a minute, I pushed the door closed and held it.

The window wasn't incredibly high, but at the angle I was holding the door, I couldn't look through it, and as soon as I let go, the door was going to burst open. I looked at the ladder going to the top of the train and thought of Jett's dream. I shouldn't go up, but where else was there to go? As soon as the pressure on the door went away, I let go and climbed as fast as I could. The door opened, but I ignored whoever must be below me.

I got to the top and pulled myself up, throwing my legs over the side. I could hear someone climbing behind me. This was great. At least the top was wider than I'd always pictured in my head. I stood and walked fast but carefully across the top of the train. If I could remember how many cars back the dining car was, I could go stomp on it, and when Jett heard the noise, he would probably figure out I was up there.

There wasn't much chance anyone would miss me moving across the top. My boots were making plenty of noise. I didn't want to run and fall on the wet, slippery surface. The rain was barely a drizzle, but it had been coming down hard only an hour ago.

The steps behind me caused me to grit my teeth. I couldn't keep moving, or I would eventually run off the front. I stomped extra hard as I walked, hoping someone would alert the engineer and the train would stop. Running wasn't an option.

I spun around, and my mouth turned down when I saw Vonna standing there in a black hoodie. Most of my fear disappeared.

"Vonna? Really?" I asked. I'd expected it to be Keith. Vonna wouldn't be hard to take in a fight. Her black hair was covered under her hood.

She stopped about eight feet in front of me, her glare cold and unwavering. "You should have minded your own business."

"And you are going to what?" I asked. "Push me from a train moving slower than I can walk? You know everyone on the train knows someone is up here. It's not like our steps have been quiet. If I disappear, everyone will know it was you, and I won't disappear because there is no way you can take me."

I was talking confidently, and I couldn't guarantee my Zumba workouts made me stronger than she was, but she didn't look like someone who could fight.

"In about one minute, the train is going to stop, and people will be up here. What's your move?" I desperately hoped she wasn't going to fight. Falling might not kill us, but it wouldn't do us any good either. Neither one of us was James Bond, and this could get bad really fast.

"Give me the bag."

"Why?"

"Someone planted it in my stuff. I need to get rid of it."

"Yeah, that might ruin your career. You should have gone to the FBI instead of trying to get rid of it. What's in it?"

"I don't know! Just give it to me," she demanded.

The train stopped, and I raised my brows. "Make a smart choice."

"Give me the bag!"

"Then what? Everything goes back to normal?" I could see Jett on the roof, hurrying toward us. "It won't."

Vonna looked over her shoulder and frowned, then looked back at me. "The evidence is in your pocket, not mine. Everyone will believe me when I tell them I was trying to stop you." She charged forward, and I dropped to the roof. Instead of plowing into me like she must have intended, she tripped over me and fell on her stomach. She kicked me in the shoulder as she fell, but I barely noticed.

I scooted away from her, ignoring the water seeping into my jeans. Vonna pushed herself onto her hands and knees. I thought about jumping on her, but any struggle up here was risky. I didn't dare take my eyes off her, but I could hear Jett getting closer. Vonna scooted back, but before she could stand, Jett had stepped past me and grabbed her arm and pulled her to her feet.

"You can't do anything!" Vonna said. "You don't have any authority here."

"That doesn't mean I'm going to let you attack someone."

I stood and looked behind me. Agents Archer and Blake were making their way toward us.

Vonna slapped Jett's hand, and he grabbed both of her arms and twisted them behind her.

"What's going on?" Agent Archer said when they came up to us.

I took a deep breath. "I saw Vonna throw a plastic baggie off the train. I got off to retrieve it, then couldn't get back inside the train because the door was locked. Vonna rammed the door into me, so I climbed up here. She wants me to give the bag to her. She said someone put it in her stuff to frame her."

"That's not true," Vonna said, struggling against Jett. Her black hair was in her face now. "I saw her come out here, so I followed her to make sure she didn't get hurt. That wouldn't be good for the show."

"Can I have the bag?" Agent Archer asked me. He pulled a plastic glove from his pocket and pulled it on. I handed it to him. He held it up. "What is it?"

I shrugged.

He turned to Vonna. "Are you going to tell me what it is?"

"It's not mine!" Vonna said. "Someone stuck it in my bag. I swear it wasn't me."

"Let's get off here," he said. Agent Blake took Vonna's arms from Jett, and we all walked carefully across the train.

I wasn't sure what the agents did with Vonna, but Jett and I returned to our room. Boyd and José were waiting inside.

"What happened?" José asked.

"My dream," Jett said, frowning at me.

"That was Ivy on the roof?" Boyd laughed. "Not that it's surprising."

"I didn't plan to go up there," I said, rummaging through my things for some dry clothes. "I didn't have anywhere else to go. I can't believe Vonna followed me."

"It was Vonna?" Boyd said. "I didn't expect that."

"But we already knew she was up to something," José pointed out.

"Yeah, but Vonna doesn't look like she could take anyone down. I'm surprised she would follow Ivy."

"I don't know what her plan was," I said. "She was improvising. She must have known I'd followed her, and she probably saw me pick up the baggie from the window. I bet she panicked and didn't think it through."

"New rule," Jett said. "No going out of the train unless it's stopped at a station."

I smiled. "I'll try."

Boyd chuckled. "I hope I'm still alive to watch the two of you if you ever get married. I can imagine Ivy, eight months pregnant, jumping on the back of a bank robber and Jett trying to give her more rules."

I wrinkled my nose. Jett sat back on the bench, then covered his face with his hands and groaned.

"Thanks a lot." Jett glared at Boyd. "Now I have something else to have nightmares about."

"Don't worry about that," José said. "If it ever comes to that, I'll go with Ivy and jump on anyone she wants me to. She can delegate."

José and Boyd laughed, but Jett just stared at them.

Boyd's eyes sparkled. "Then she'll have a baby strapped to her back while she's hiding in a closet, eavesdropping on someone."

Jett looked like he might be sick.

"Knock it off, you two," I said. "I would never take a baby into danger." I was going to say we had only been dating for a month, so worrying about things like that was crazy, but I had a feeling we wouldn't waste a lot of time before we got married. We'd jokingly talked about getting married before we had officially gone on a date.

Jett didn't look assured.

I grabbed my dry clothes and left to change. With luck, this would all be tied up today. I wondered if the show would go on without Vonna. She was the host, but I wasn't sure who the mastermind behind it all was. I would guess Theo. He was the one people seemed to listen to. Vonna wouldn't go down quietly. She would probably take Keith down with her. I wondered what Fiona would do. Would she keep cooking if her son was arrested?

Chapter 11

We arrived at a station early the next day. No one was allowed off the train, and we all waited to see what would happen. Some people thought the contest would be canceled, but others thought it would go on without Vonna. We were all in the passenger seats, waiting for instructions. This was the first time we'd sat in here. The seats were comfortable, and we could sit where we wanted since there weren't regular passengers.

"What do you think will happen?" I asked Jett.

"Huh?" he said. He'd been staring out at the people passing by with a blank expression.

"Do you think *The Culinary Roadshow* will continue?"

He shook his head like he was coming out of a fog. "Um—probably. I talked to some people, and Theo is the one behind it all. He put out money for it, and it was his idea. Vonna wasn't hired until the show was about to start."

"Why would she want to draw more attention to it?"

"It would be good for her career if the show was picked up by a network. More eyes on her and everything else."

I nodded. I wondered what was happening with Keith. Vonna must not have ratted him out yet because he was still sitting in here with the rest of the crew.

Jett had seemed distracted since yesterday, but I wasn't sure I wanted to know why. He kept glancing at me and frowning, so I wondered if Boyd's teasing from yesterday was still bothering him. I didn't know how to approach that topic, but ignoring it wouldn't make it go away.

"Are you alright?" I finally asked.

He grinned. "Yep."

"Liar. What's wrong?"

He sighed and laced his fingers with mine. "Our relationship is the most important thing in the world to me."

"But?"

"I can't get what Boyd said out of my head. I keep picturing you smacking someone over the head with a baby stroller or a diaper bag. It's stupid, but it's stressing me out. Last night, I googled some stuff and almost decided we should move to Iceland."

I tilted my head. "Iceland?"

"It's one of the safest countries in the world. You wouldn't run into these crazy things there."

"We aren't moving to Iceland."

He blew out a breath. "I know. How about Ireland?"

I touched his cheek. "We aren't moving. We have jobs in Muddy Creek."

"Yeah, but I know you. If a mystery pops up, you can't ignore it."

"If we get married—"

"When, not if," he said, cutting me off.

I smiled. "Life changes, Jett. Right now, I live with my cat above a diner. The town is small, and there isn't a lot to do. I imagine having kids changes a person's life and priorities. I'm not going to be in a car chase in a minivan with four kids in the back."

He raised his eyebrow. "Four kids, huh?"

"Fine. Five. I can compromise."

He dropped my hand and put his arm over my shoulders. "Can you really picture me driving a minivan?"

"Too cool for a minivan? You can drive your silly Cybertruck, and I'll drive the minivan. Deal?"

He chuckled. "Deal." He gave me a crooked smile. "A minivan is definitely big enough to carry a dog."

I groaned. "You said you don't have time for a dog."

"But if I have a minivan full of little people, they would help, right?"

"That's always the flawed theory."

"Don't you want your kids to have a dog?"

I sighed. "You know I'm a cat person."

"Can't you be a cat and a dog person?"

"I'm not sure that's allowed. I'm pretty sure there are rules about that."

He laughed. "We can discuss it again once we see how responsible our kids are."

I leaned into him and put my arm around him. Sometimes not having an armrest was a good thing. "I love you."

"I love you too." He seemed more at peace now. I was glad I'd decided to talk.

Agent Archer poked his head into the room, and his eyes scanned the crowd. When he saw us, he motioned for us to come. We stood and made our way down the aisle. When we entered the next car, Agent Archer stood there with Agent Blake and Theo.

"We've been talking," he said. "Agent Blake will get off the train and take Vonna into custody. She isn't giving us anything to go on. She won't admit anything, but we can still take her in for attacking you, if nothing else."

I nodded.

"*The Culinary Roadshow* rented the train, and now that it's been stopped for multiple days, it's behind schedule. The train can't continue for longer than it was rented."

Theo cleared his throat. "We were hoping to continue the contest in Muddy Creek at Sue's Diner. The train can get us to Newton, Kansas, and we would take a bus to Wichita, then get an Uber or something similar to take us there."

I nodded. "That would be fine, but we would have to do the contests after hours, and I only have two ovens. Well, and the one in my apartment upstairs. It doesn't cook as evenly, but I could use that one."

"I'll come and continue the investigation," Agent Archer said. He turned to Theo. "Feel free to go ask all your crew and contestants if they are alright with this."

Theo nodded and headed into the passenger car.

"I thought you called us in here to tell me not to follow people and climb on trains," I said.

Both agents laughed.

"We figured you already knew that," Agent Archer said.

I was a little surprised they didn't seem annoyed. I'd expected a huge lecture and possibly even threats. All my expectations of the FBI had been wrong. I'd expected them to wear suits, and so far, I'd only seen them in dark jeans and button-up shirts. They also smiled more than I would have thought.

"Is there anywhere in Muddy Creek all the crew can stay?" I asked Jett. "I didn't think about that. The B&B isn't very big, so it won't hold everyone."

"We can talk to José," Jett said. "His house is old, but it's got a lot of extra rooms. A few can stay with me. I have two empty rooms. I'm sure we can find enough space if the crew doesn't mind being separated."

Agent Archer rubbed his chin. "It would probably be smart to split up all the teams. If Vonna wasn't working alone, people could still be in danger. Put the people from Calico Café at the B&B and Colby somewhere else."

"All the other places are with our team, though," I said.

"Right, hmm. How many rooms are at the B&B?"

Jett narrowed his eyes and looked thoughtful. "I would say ten to twelve."

"Do you think some are in use?"

"I can call the owner and ask. There aren't usually many people. Muddy Creek isn't a place most people go on vacation."

"It might be best to only use the B&B and have most of the crew stay in Wichita and drive over for the filming. I can stay there with Colby and the other group. The judges can stay there as well, and I can put up cameras. Sheriff Malone will have jurisdiction again, so he can help with the rest of the case."

Jett clenched his jaw and nodded.

"Can you send me the number for the B&B? I should talk to the owner so they don't feel like we're taking over."

"I'll text it to you," Jett said, pulling his phone from his pocket.

"Great. I need to go check some things." He left the room, and I waited for Jett to text the number.

Jett put the phone back in his pocket and sighed.

"I'm sorry," I said, putting my arms around his waist.

"Why?"

"You never get a real vacation. Now you're going to have to help with this investigation."

"It's fine. I'm sure Agent Archer will want to do most of it. I can probably get Deputy Ledford to help while we're doing the show."

I groaned. "Not Ledford."

"I thought the two of you were getting along better since you saved him?"

I shrugged. "Better, but not great. Plus, I haven't butted into his work since then. That might make it look like we're getting along because we aren't dealing with each other."

Jett laughed. "Ledford is actually growing on me. I was ready to send him back to Chicago or wherever he came from, but he's eased my workload."

The train moved forward, and I sighed with relief. I was glad we were going to Muddy Creek. Being on a train was only fun for so long.

"I'm going to go sit in the passenger section," I said. I need a few minutes without Boyd trying to make me play cards.

"Alright," Jett said, giving me a squeeze. "I think I'll see if Agent Archer will clue me in on anything he might be keeping quiet. If he wants me to work with him, I should know everything."

We went our separate ways, and I ended up in a window seat, watching Kansas pass before my eyes.

"Can I sit?" Fiona asked.

"Sure."

Fiona wore a gold dress and gold shoes. We weren't filming today, so I wasn't sure why she was so dressed up. Maybe she dressed up every day. I'd been wearing nicer clothes than usual since I went on my shopping spree. I would never admit it, but seeing Jett's eyes light up every time I wore something new was exciting.

"This is quite the mess we've all gotten into," Fiona said, pulling a tissue from her pocket and blowing her nose. "And now I'm having allergies. I can't handle this weather. I'm glad Vonna is off the train. That woman was driving me crazy."

"I didn't deal with her a lot," I said.

"She's a tricky one. I know she was trying to get Keith to do her bidding. She was always getting him to come walk around with her. I'm glad he's smart enough to see through a woman like her."

I pressed my lips together and didn't say anything. I was almost sure Keith had done something he shouldn't, even if it was only replacing Gavin's vanilla.

She pushed her brown hair over her shoulder. "She was always finding reasons to touch his arm or bump into him. I know her type, and I'm glad Keith isn't swayed by people like her."

I definitely wouldn't tell her about the kiss I witnessed between Keith and Vonna.

"What does Keith do?" I asked. "Work at your restaurant?"

"Yes. I pay him plenty. He's second-in-command."

I couldn't imagine that. Not unless he was being paid to play on his phone.

"Does he date?" I asked, realizing that probably wasn't an appropriate question.

She sighed. "Girls these days are so picky. They think they can find Mr. Perfect. He meets a lot of girls online, but it rarely goes for more than one date. It's too bad for them. Keith is a great catch."

I didn't think Vonna was actually interested in Keith. My guess was that she was just trying to get him to do things. Vonna had too much going for her, and Keith didn't. I might be judging him too harshly. I didn't really know what he's like in his normal life. He wasn't bad looking, just average, but I couldn't imagine dating someone who was glued to their phone.

"What do you think about finishing the contest at your diner? I just heard that's the new plan."

"I'm fine with it."

"Of course. You get home-court advantage."

"I'll be the only one not using the diner kitchen. That gives me a disadvantage because my oven isn't the same grade. It's fine, but it doesn't cook as evenly." Great. Now I sounded defensive.

"I'm sure it's fine. It does seem a little unfair, but I'll let it slide since there isn't a choice."

Jett walked in, and his eyes scanned the room. He came up to us. "Did you see where Agent Archer went? He's not in his room."

"He didn't pass by here," I said.

"Do you feel intimidated by the FBI?" Fiona asked.

Jett shrugged. "Why would I? We both have the same goals. I appreciate all they do."

She laughed. "You really do have the same goals. I saw the way Agent Archer was watching Ivy yesterday."

My eyes narrowed, and my mouth turned down. What was she talking about? He hadn't paid me any more attention than anyone else.

Jett just smiled. "I'm not worried about that."

"You don't worry about other men moving in on your territory?"

"Ivy and I have something special. I'm not worried. I'm going to go look in the other cars." He turned and walked through the back door.

Fiona smiled as she watched him leave.

"Agent Archer doesn't watch me," I said, "but you seem to watch Jett."

She laughed. "Who wouldn't? It's good you two are both so secure with each other because every woman who sees that man is going to watch him."

I raised my brow. "You know he's only two years older than Keith?"

"No harm in looking."

I went back to looking out the window. I wasn't going to let myself get into some crazy jealous fit. Fiona was old enough to be Jett's mom, and it was like Jett said. We had something special. I smiled at the memory of him saying it.

"Keith needs to find girls who are less superficial," Fiona said, either not noticing or caring that I felt awkward. "He doesn't have the wow factor like the sheriff, and girls aren't willing to see what a man has to offer if she isn't enamored with him immediately."

"Vonna seemed to like him," I said. "I saw them kissing." I bit the inside of my cheek. I'd only said that because Fiona annoyed me, and that wasn't the way to do things.

I could feel Fiona's eyes burning into me. "I don't believe you."

I shrugged. "I think you do." I stood and squeezed past her. Staying in the same car with her would only lead to more trouble. It wasn't my best moment, and I tried not to enjoy the look of shock on Fiona's face.

Chapter 12

J ett and Agent Archer stood with their backs to us at the train station in Newton, talking and directing people as they got off the train. I stepped off with José at my side and Fiona and Boyd behind me. I hadn't spoken to her in the day and a half it took us to cross Kansas.

"He really makes those jeans look good," Fiona said, leaning close to me and pointing at Jett.

"He does, doesn't he?" I said, not letting her rile me.

"Thanks," José said, grinning mischievously. "I work out."

"I think she was talking about me," Boyd said.

I smiled, and Fiona rolled her eyes and stormed over to Jett and Agent Archer.

José chuckled. "What was that all about?"

"I don't know. I haven't had any problems with Fiona, but we might have had a falling-out the other day. Now she's trying to make me jealous or mad. I'm not sure which."

"Hmm. Is that why she's holding Jett's arm?"

I grinned. "Probably. I don't get it. If she thinks I'll feel threatened by her attention to Jett, she's wrong. It does irritate me, though."

Boyd smiled and walked over to Fiona. I couldn't hear what he said, but she dropped Jett's arm and stomped off.

"What do you think he said?" I asked.

José smiled and shook his head. "With Boyd, it's anyone's guess."

By the time we all got to Muddy Creek, I was ready to go to bed. Most of the crew was in Wichita, and they would come tomorrow for filming. I'd texted Barbra to let her know I was coming, so she'd returned home. We had led everyone who came with us to the B&B, where the rooms were waiting for them.

Jett walked me home. We went into my apartment, and I called for Creepers. He walked into the room and looked at me, then walked out again.

"Ohhhh! He's mad at you," Jett said.

I sighed. "I think you're right."

"To be fair, I'd be mad if you left me and went on an adventure without me."

"I know how to get back in his good graces." We went into the kitchen, and I popped the top of a can of wet food. Creepers came tearing into the room, meowing. I gave him the food and waited to pet him. I knew how his priorities worked.

"What's going on with Fiona?" Jett asked. She's been giving you some dirty looks. And what's with Boyd? He came up at the train station and said, 'If the sheriff is too busy to help you cross the street, I'm here for you.' That made her fume. I was glad it made her let go of my arm."

I giggled. "I love Boyd. That was mean, though."

"I thought the two of you got along?"

I shrugged. "We did, but we had a—bad conversation, I guess. It started when she told you that Agent Archer watches me. I told her he didn't, and I might have mentioned how she watches you. That was something I probably should have kept to myself."

Jett wrinkled his nose. "Fiona watches me?"

I nodded and smiled. "She also said you look good in your jeans."

He ran a hand over his face. "Gross. She's old enough to be my mom."

"She was right, though."

He held up his hand. "Stop trying to make me blush."

His neck was red, so I decided to stop teasing him. "I'm looking forward to this contest ending. I wonder how many days it will take."

"I don't know. I told Agent Archer all about our suspicions and everything we knew. He already had his eye on Keith. He's pretty sure Vonna was using him."

"I'm surprised she hasn't turned him in."

"I'm not. Things will be worse for her if it turns out she got other people to do her bidding. She probably doesn't want anything to get out about her relationship with Keith. That might be more embarrassing to her than all the other stuff. Right now, all they have on her is that she tried to throw out evidence and tried to attack you. She could end up getting off."

"Do you think she will?"

"Probably."

I yawned. "You should probably go. We have an early morning tomorrow, and you need sleep."

He grinned. "So you're kicking me out?"

I put my arms around his neck and kissed his chin. "Don't think of it as kicking you out. Think of it as taking care of you."

The following morning was chaotic. Camera people were all over my apartment. Since we couldn't bake until the diner was closed, Theo wanted us to redo some of our small interview sessions. The video quality on the train wasn't as good as he liked, so they were setting up in my living room.

I ran down to the diner to check on Carrie and Anton. Everything looked just like we left it.

"How have things been?" I asked.

Carrie looked up from scrambling eggs. "We've been fine. It's been a little rough without José, but we're managing."

"No problems at all," Anton said, whisking something in a bowl.

"I think José plans on helping as much as he can today," I said. "I'm surprised he isn't here now."

The back door opened, and José came in. "Hey, everyone. Sorry I'm late. I can help until they need me for an interview." He looked at Carrie. "Command me, and I will obey."

Carrie blushed. "You're the manager."

I hid a smile. The more I watched, the more I was sure Carrie had a thing for José that she wasn't ready to tell him about.

"I don't know what's going on," he said. "What do you need?"

"Someone needs to make dessert for the lunch and dinner crowd," she said.

"I'm on it," he said, going into the pantry.

Livy rushed in, her red ponytail flying. "A ton of people just came in! We're going to need help."

I looked out the window from the kitchen to the dining area. It was full of people from Theo's crew.

"I can help Livy take orders, then cook," Anton offered.

"No, I'll get the orders," I said, grabbing an ordering pad. I went out and took a table. It was weird to wait on the people who had been doing my makeup, but they were all polite about it. Once the rush was over, I went back up to my room.

If the crew ate every meal here, cleaning the kitchen in time for the show at night would be hard. On the other hand, it was good business. After the morning rush, I went back up to my apartment.

When I went into the sitting room, someone put a finger to their mouth and pointed. Boyd was sitting on my recliner, talking to the camera. I quietly shut the door and stood in the corner, watching.

Boyd wore an untucked red-and-blue Hawaiian shirt and bright green shoes. "Here's the thing about cows," he was saying. "Cows like other cows. They like to make friends, and they can even have best friends. I had a lot of cows over the years, and they are interesting creatures. I had two named Mavis and Hattie. Those two were as thick as thieves. If I gave something to one of them, I had to give the same thing to the other, or they would both nip at me.

"One day, I came in the house after a long day on the farm and found Mavis and Hattie in my kitchen eating apples off the table. It took me over an hour to get them out and another hour to sanitize and clean everything. I never would have gotten them out if it wasn't for my pig, Jasper. Pigs are smart and as good as dogs for most things. He ran around trying to herd them out."

"Have you ever had dogs?" the interviewer asked.

"Sure, but I'd take a guard pig over a dog any day. If any unwelcome visitors come, they're more likely to run away from a charging pig."

"But dogs are cuddly."

"Sure, but so are pigs, and they love a good belly rub."

I managed to stand and listen to the rest of Boyd's interview without laughing. When he was finished, they wanted to talk to me. This was the worst thing about the competition. They didn't even want to know about baking. They wanted to know personal things that I didn't want to share with the world. Thankfully, they settled on me talking about growing up in Arizona.

By the time evening came, I was tired from all the people coming in and out of my home. The contest started in the diner kitchen, where Theo announced that we would be baking two types of muffins. They decided to make things a little less complicated since Colby was baking by himself. He looked relieved.

The cameramen were divided, so some stayed in the diner and some came up to my place.

"What type should we make?" José asked, scanning our ingredients. Theo had bought all the ingredients to prevent anyone from altering them.

"I don't care," I said. "What do you think?"

"Lemon poppy seed and pumpkin chocolate chip? We want to look like we put some effort in, and muffins are pretty basic, so that might get us points for not doing anything too easy."

"Sounds good."

Jett grabbed the mixer from the counter and brought it to the small island. It felt crowded with the four of us and the cameraman in the small area.

"Boyd and Ivy, do the pumpkin, and Jett and I will do the lemon," José said.

I love making pumpkin chocolate chip muffins. I hadn't done it since November, but I'd made them so many times the recipe was burned into my memory. Since pumpkin wasn't one of the ingredients Theo bought, I had to show him the can from my pantry so he could inspect it. I think he was secretly worried the unfortunate pie incident had been meant for him and not Gavin.

We met in the dining area once all the muffins were finished and cool. The judges sat at a booth with a cameraman standing on the booth seat in front of them.

Bianca looked bored as she studied the muffins in front of her. Her hair was twisted into a fancy bun that looked like it would take ages to do. She picked up one of Colby's blueberry muffins and nibbled a piece from the corner. She moved onto his banana muffin and did the same. Theo took a regular-sized bite of each one.

Bianca looked at Theo for guidance.

"They're both passable," Theo said. "The blueberry is too crumbly, and the banana is too mushy. Nothing too bad, but nothing impressive."

Colby took a deep breath and nodded.

Next, the judges tried ours.

"Both are perfect," Theo said. "I would pay for a muffin like these."

I smiled at José. He looked relieved. Bianca didn't seem to be talking today. This show was going to flop. There was almost nothing interesting about it unless you counted Gavin dying. It would probably bore anyone watching it.

The judges ate Fiona's and gave her good reviews. Fiona's eyes sparkled as she looked at me. I wasn't sure how our relationship had gone bad so fast. I still had to deal with her for a bit longer because they hadn't done her interview today, so she would be up in my apartment later tonight.

Everything wrapped up, and people began going their separate ways.

"Let's go up for that last interview," Theo said.

"Come," I mouthed to Jett. We went up to my apartment and stood off to the side while Fiona situated herself on the recliner.

"We need something interesting," Theo said. "I'm afraid our ratings will either do really well or bomb this season. I'm hoping for the first option. Do you have anything catchy or controversial you can say?"

"Hmm," Fiona said. "Can I be interviewed with the sheriff?"

"No," Jett said.

She smiled at him. "Why? Scared?"

"Yep."

"Come on," Theo said. "The show needs something."

"Gavin isn't enough?" I asked. "It's going to be all over the news."

"Come on. I don't bite," Fiona said.

Jett looked at me, and I shrugged. I didn't see anything good coming from it, but I didn't have a good argument either.

"I'll do it, but I'm not going to lie or try to make anyone look good," Jett finally said.

"Okay, move the cameras and put Jett and Fiona on the couch," Theo said.

Everything was moved, and Jett ended up sitting next to Fiona.

Fiona smiled into the camera. "I believe that competitions are good times to get to know the people you are working against. It's a good time to make connections and make lifelong friends. I've gotten to know Sheriff Jett here and feel we have a great connection."

Jett moved his jaw to the side and raised his brow. "We've only talked twice."

"Which makes the connection even more unique," she said. "It's like we already know each other. I feel that way about everyone on the show." She put her hand on Jett's knee, and he scooted farther away. "You remind me of someone," she said, looking at him.

"You remind me of my grandma, except a little creepy."

Theo snorted and turned to the corner, where his shoulders shook. I figured he was either laughing or crying.

Fiona's glare could sour milk. "You're ridiculous, you know that? Forget this. Start it over without him here."

Theo turned and shook his head. "Nope, we're keeping it."

Fiona scowled at Jett. "This is all fake, you know? People don't actually believe it. It's not like you couldn't play along. It's what people want to see."

"I don't want to see it," Jett said. "I don't want you hitting on me in real life or on a show."

"People would watch the show just to see a relationship between us."

"I have a relationship."

"I just told you, this stuff isn't real. It's for the ratings!"

"That's not a good enough reason for me. I am the sheriff of Muddy Creek. I believe in the old-fashioned values of being a good person and taking care of people. I'm not about scandals and ratings. Being true to yourself and those you love are what's important."

"You're just saying that because your little girlfriend is over there in the corner."

"It wouldn't matter if no one else was in the room. There would never be anything between us."

"Just get out of here!" she yelled, picking up my plant and flinging it at Jett. He leaned slightly to the left, and it crashed to the floor, making a mess of dirt. I didn't really like the plant, but now I was going to have to clean up.

"You can't kick my boyfriend out of my apartment," I said. I ignored the camera as it turned onto me. Were they still recording? "You're welcome to leave, though."

Fiona stood and stomped from the house, slamming the door as she left.

Theo laughed softly. "That's the third time Fiona's fallen apart in an interview."

"Really?" I asked. "I thought she was normal and confident until the past few days."

"She must have hidden it from you. Gavin actually threatened to get a restraining order against her if she didn't leave him alone. And that was after the first day."

"I didn't see them interact at all."

"She snuck into his room on the train. He said she was going through his things, but she said she was just in there waiting to talk to him. Then at her interview, she talked about what an idiot Gavin was."

"Did you tell this to Agent Archer?" I asked.

"Yep. I told him everything I'd seen. Let's get cleaned up. We have a break tomorrow, so we should all take advantage and get good rest."

The crew all packed up and left. Jett went to the coat closet and pulled out the vacuum.

"Don't worry about that," I said. "I can get it."

He plugged it in. "She threw it at me. That makes it my mess. Besides, I like to help you, so sit down and put up your feet."

I smiled. Jett was the greatest. Now I had time to think about Fiona and why she would have been in Gavin's room.

Chapter 13

Creepers and I sat in the window seat in my bedroom, listening to the rain. Creepers snuggled against me, and I ran my hand over his gray fur. It was still early, but I should be getting ready to help in the diner. If we didn't film until tomorrow, there was no reason to waste today. I'm not usually lazy, but rain makes me want to sit and listen and not move. I waited a few more minutes, then put Creepers down and got ready for the day.

When I got downstairs, José already had the kitchen ready for the breakfast crowd. Theo told us to expect all the crew staying in town to eat at the diner every day. They could eat at the B&B, but the breakfast there was more like a continental breakfast than anything sustaining.

"I'll get going on the desserts," I said, plugging in the mixer. "Are Carrie and Anton coming in today?"

"Yeah. I was going to tell them to take a day off, but since we're getting so many people while filming, we'll need them. I'll give them lighter schedules when this is over."

A few minutes later, Carrie came in. "Hello. It's good to have you two back. You know I love Anton, but man. He's been so distracted since he and Livy started dating. Every time she comes in with an order, they have to smile at each other. I'm just glad he's over *The Princess Bride* thing."

"I agree," José said.

"What's that?" I asked.

"It was annoying. Livy's favorite movie is *The Princess Bride*. Once Anton learned that, he was unbearable."

Carrie nodded. "Every time she came in and said she needed a hot chocolate or something, he would say, 'As you wish.' It was cute the first few times, and then it got annoying."

"Where was I?" I asked.

"My guess?" José shrugged. "Probably out smooching Jett somewhere. You haven't been around as much as usual the last month."

I could feel my face turn red. "Sorry about that. I wasn't with Jett most of the time because he was on duty, but I haven't been in the diner as much as I should. I think I read five books last month."

"It's fine," José assured. "You're the owner. You don't have to work here."

"I know, but I want to."

"Hey, everyone," Boyd greeted, coming in the back door. "Anything exciting today?"

"Not so far," I said.

"Jett told me about Fiona. I bet she ends up getting arrested before this thing is over."

I laughed. "For what?"

"Dunno. She seems the type, though. I told Jett to stay far away from her and to carry bear mace. She's the type who will cause problems."

José chuckled. "Bear mace? I'm pretty sure Jett has a gun."

"I don't know how you all can cook so much. It would drive me crazy if I had to cook half as much as you all do."

"I love baking," I said.

"Cooking isn't my passion, but I don't mind it," Carrie said. "I always told my mom I was going to marry a man who could cook because I hated it when I was young."

I looked discreetly over at José and smiled when I saw him whisk the pancake batter harder than was necessary. I wondered if José would ever ask Carrie out. I wasn't sure how many relationships the diner could handle between my employees.

It wasn't long before the diner was full. When Theo came in, he asked me to come talk to him. I went and sat across from him and Bianca.

"We decided to tell the teams one thing they can do to-day to prepare for tomorrow. You need to find a cookbook and bring it to the competition. It can't belong to you or anyone in your family. It needs to be one that you have never used before. You don't need to know why. You just need to bring it."

"Okay," I said, trying to think of who I could borrow one from. I wondered if the library had cookbooks. That might be a good place to start. Checking out a cookbook sounded weird, but almost everything in the Muddy Creek library was donated, so it wasn't impossible.

As soon as there was a lull at the diner, I walked to the library. Brian, the librarian, was sitting at his desk reading a book. He was smiling and didn't seem to notice I was there.

"Hi, Brian," I said, smiling when he jumped.

He put a hand to his chest. "Ivy! You just about scared me to death."

"Good book?"

He rubbed the back of his neck and grinned slightly. "It's a graphic novel for fifth graders. It just got donated, so I wanted to read it and make sure it was really age appropriate. You never know what you'll get these days, even with kid books."

"You seemed sucked in."

"It's stupid, just like you would expect for the audience they're going for, but yes, it's hooked me. Now I'll have to get the other nine or ten books in the series because any kid who checks this out will want the rest.”

“It’s not just that you want to read the rest?” I teased.

He grinned. “I’ll never admit it. Can I help you with something today, or are you just here to chat?”

“I know this is weird, but do you have any cookbooks?”

He ran his fingers through his curly black hair. “Yes, but they’re all beat up and old. I don’t think anyone has ever checked one out. I think Opal donated them when the library first opened.”

“It doesn’t matter. I just need a cookbook I’ve never used before.”

“For the show?”

I nodded. “I bet they’ll have us make a random recipe from it.”

“Well, follow me, and I’ll show you what I have.”

We walked to the back of the library, and Brian pointed at the bottom shelf. “I think I have about five down there.”

I dropped to my knees and found them immediately. They were all tall and stood out. I grabbed a red-and-white-checkered book and opened it randomly in the middle. The page was covered in stains from spilled ingredients.

“It looks like someone used it a lot,” I said. “Are you sure this is from Opal? Opal strikes me as a neat freak. This looks more like something Barbra would have.” I started helping Barbra unclutter her house a few months ago, and we still weren't finished.

"I'm not sure why I even keep them. I guess for times like this."

"I bet the other teams will come in. I doubt they sell cookbooks anywhere in Muddy Creek. There can't be a lot of demand."

"Probably not. You better make sure you take the best one then."

"The other teams could use mine if they need to. I have two or three. I think José has a huge collection at home."

"Hello? Is anyone here?" someone called from the front of the library. It sounded like Fiona. I cringed.

"You should be at the front to shush her," I said, trying to smile. "Watch out. She's a little scary."

Brian laughed and left me with the books. I would hide here until Fiona left, but Brian would probably lead her over any minute. I grabbed the cleanest book and stood and went to the front.

Brian was talking to Fiona. He took the book and my library card and scanned it while he told Fiona she would have to have a library card. Fiona ignored him and glared at me.

"You can use one of my cookbooks," I told her. I really didn't like to have bad feelings with people. Nothing good ever came from it. If she had never involved Jett in any of our conversations, I was sure we would still be fine.

"So you can sabotage me?" she asked.

"No, so you have a cookbook. You can go grab one from the kitchen right now if you want. I won't even touch it. I'll text one of my people and have them show you where they are."

Fiona's eyes narrowed, and she turned and walked briskly from the building.

"She seems friendly," Brian said, grinning.

"I'm trying to be nice, but she's making it hard. She likes to drool over Jett and his nice-fitting jeans."

Brian burst into laughter. "I can see how that would give you issues. How is Jett taking that?"

I smiled. "She tried to hit on him on camera yesterday, and he told her she reminded him of his grandma."

"Ouch."

"I don't think he's in the mood to deal with her."

A dog barked. It was a small yappy sound.

"Did you get a dog?" I asked. Brian had given me Creepers and struck me as a cat-only kind of guy.

Brian sighed. "My brother's dog had puppies, and I somehow let him talk me into taking one. You know I have five cats? It's not going well. The puppy is happy and ready to give some love, but the cats aren't having it. I'm keeping him in my office here because the cats are too terrified at the moment, and I thought they needed some time at the house without him. They're all hiding."

"That's not good."

"Nope. I'm going to try to find him a home because it's not working."

"Can I see him?"

"Sure." We walked over, and Brian opened the door. A white ball of fluff came barreling out, and Brian scooped him up.

"Oh my goodness," I said, taking the puppy when Brian offered him. "That is the cutest thing I've ever seen!" He licked my face, which would usually disgust me, but he was so adorable.

"He likes you. You should keep him," Brian said. "Please keep him."

I laughed. "Creepers would never forgive me. What kind is he?"

"A Maltese. They don't get very big. He's almost potty trained."

"What's his name?"

"I haven't named him."

I rubbed his head, and he tried to lick my hands. "Jett wants a dog. Can I take him and show it to him?"

"Sure. I doubt this is the type of dog Jett has in mind, though."

I cradled the wiggly dog in my arms and walked over to Jett's house. I kicked the door a few times because I couldn't use either hand.

The door opened, and Jett peeked out. He opened it wider when he saw me. "Hey, Ivs." He looked at the puppy. "What is that?"

I rolled my eyes. "A dog."

"What are you doing with it?"

"Showing it to you. Isn't he adorable? He's Brian's, but Brian can't keep him."

"I hope you aren't thinking about taking him."

"I thought you wanted a dog."

"A dog, yes. This is as close to being a cat as you can get and still miss the mark completely." He took the dog from my hands, and it immediately began licking him.

"Whoa, whoa," he said with a laugh. He rubbed behind its little ears.

"Isn't it the cutest thing?"

"Yeah, but it's a yappy dog. They bark at everything."

"But he's cute."

"I thought you didn't want a dog?"

"I didn't, but he's so adorable."

"Creepers will hate him."

"Maybe not."

"I don't have time to train a puppy."

"I do!" Boyd said, pushing his way out the door past Jett. "I've had at least ten dogs in my lifetime. I haven't gotten another one because I'm too old for nighttime potty outings, but Jett can do that part."

Boyd took the puppy from Jett and carried him into the house. We followed. Boyd placed him on the floor of the front room and sat next to him.

"Boyd, you can't get up from the floor," I cautioned.

"Jett can pull me up." The puppy climbed on Boyd's pants and tried to chew them.

Jett crossed his arms. "Now if we don't take him, I have to be the bad guy."

"We're keeping him," Boyd said.

"When I said I wanted a dog, I meant like a collie or a husky or something bigger than this."

"But he's so cute!" I said.

Jett's eyes sparkled when he looked at the dog, but I could tell he wasn't sold.

"That isn't a good little kid dog," Jett said. "I've researched dogs, and this isn't the one you want."

"I can get it to be a kid dog," Boyd said. "It just takes patience. What should we name it?"

"Sammy?" I suggested.

Jett groaned. "Now I can't take it away from Boyd. Not Sammy. It needs to be something more terrifying."

"Stevie?"

"Nothing that ends in that sound."

"The Terminator?" Boyd suggested. "Then we can have a sign on the fence that says, Beware of the Terminator."

"Let's figure this out later," Jett said. "Tell Brian we'll take him, but not until after the contest is over."

"I'll take him over and talk to Brian," Boyd said. "Just as soon as you all pull me up off the floor."

We helped Boyd off the floor, and he left with the puppy.

"I can't believe anything can be so cute," I said as Jett shut the door.

Jett grabbed me and spun me around, pulling my arms across my stomach, and pinned me against him so I couldn't move. "That was pretty low. How was I supposed to say no to Boyd?"

I tried to look over my shoulder at him, but he had me pinned too well. I expected to be tickled at any moment because that was what usually happened when Jett trapped me like this. "You wanted a dog."

"A dog, not a rat. You know that thing will tear apart my house and probably do his business all over my floor?"

A small giggle escaped me. "I'm sorry. Brian showed him to me, and he was so fluffy and sweet."

"You don't sound repentant."

"I'm not."

He rubbed his face into my neck. "You will be when you're trying to get him and Creepers to get along."

"Can I turn so I can hug you and not myself?"

He released my arms, and I turned and put my arms around him. "If the puppy has an accident, you can call me, and I'll come clean it up."

"I'm never home. Once I've used my vacation days, Boyd will be in charge during the day. I can't believe you went from anti-dog to getting a dog that fast."

"Yeah, that's because—"

"I know. He's so cute."

Chapter 14

"Everyone has their cookbook?" Theo asked. He'd now taken over as host as well as judge.

José, Fiona, and Colby held their cookbooks in the air.

"Today, you will all turn to page thirteen of your cookbook and make something on that page. Everyone, to your places!"

I followed José up to my apartment, and Jett came after me. I was glad we got to work upstairs in my apartment instead of with the other two groups. Having Fiona glare at me all the time was uncomfortable. Once we were in the kitchen, we had to wait for the cameras to get set up.

I opened the cookbook to page thirteen. "Pretzels," I said. "That's the only recipe on the page, and it only has a few ingredients."

"What?" José asked, grabbing the book. "How are we supposed to make fancy pretzels from this?"

Theo came in. "There's something else," he said, smiling. "Only one person can work on your recipe today. Downstairs, we drew names, and Keith will represent Calico Café, and of course, Colby will represent The Velvet Pearl."

I frowned. This could be really bad, depending on who was chosen.

"Pull a name from the cup," Theo said, holding out a mug.

I grabbed a slip of paper and opened it. "Jett. Lovely." Our team gave a collective groan.

"This is going to be bad," Jett muttered, looking at the recipe.

"Everyone else has to leave the kitchen," Theo said. "Meet back in the diner kitchen in exactly two hours."

José, Boyd, and I left the room and the apartment.

"I'm going to go play with our dog," Boyd said.

"Dog?" José asked.

I took a deep breath. "Brian was trying to get rid of a dog. I was overwhelmed by its cuteness, so we agreed to take it."

"Who is we?"

"Jett and Boyd. It's more like they are taking it. I'm having serious regret. Last night, I kept thinking about how much work a puppy is."

"It'll be fine," Boyd assured.

José grinned. "Jett loves dogs, but a puppy might be too much with his job."

"This one isn't what he was thinking. It's small."

"Oh, a yapper?"

"Yep."

"He's the best dog ever," Boyd said.

José nodded. "I'm going with Boyd to see the puppy."

"I'm going for a walk," I said. "I have some things I need to think through. I'll meet you all later."

I strolled down the town square. There were so many things I wanted to think about, but I was having trouble focusing. I like to think about things before I go to sleep, but the past few nights, I fell asleep before I could have coherent thoughts.

Vonna was definitely guilty of something. My guess was she had gotten Keith to trade out the vanilla, which wasn't a huge crime. Still, there was the baggie she had tried to get rid of. Once we knew what was in that, things might make more sense. Keith's only crime might be trading the vanilla. But if that was true, why would Vonna think he'd gone too far with something?

This was pointless. I was only thinking of things I'd already thought of a hundred times before. Theo said Fiona had been snooping in Gavin's room. What was her place in all this? She probably didn't know what Keith and Vonna were up to. She'd been angry when I said I'd seen them together.

There was also Colby. He might have a motive. Colby didn't seem to like Gavin but valued the knowledge he was getting from him. Killing Gavin hadn't been a good thing for Colby because now he had to do everything on his own, and he didn't have the knowledge or experience to beat Fiona. Of course, he could have done it by accident if he'd been trying to target the judges.

It was possible that the entire thing had been an accident. Someone might have been trying to make someone sick and not kill them, which was still bad but not the same thing.

Theo and Bianca could be involved, but what would they benefit if Gavin died? They could have motives like Vonna. They might have wanted better ratings for the show and thought a bit of controversy might help.

Several crew members could have hated Gavin or the judges for various reasons. It seemed reasonable to believe that the unripe berries and crushed cashew shells were for the judges. I kept forgetting that Gavin shouldn't have even eaten the pie.

I found myself standing in front of the B&B. I went to the door and opened it slowly. I peeked in and didn't see Ms. Medley. She didn't seem to like me even though we've had very little contact. It might not be me. She might not like anyone. She runs the B&B.

The desk in the small front lobby was empty. A bell sat on the desk, but I wouldn't ring it if I didn't have to. I leaned over the table to see the list I knew would be there. Keith Huxley was in room three. I walked down the hall that led to the rooms and paused at door three. I looked both ways, then tried the doorknob.

"Looking for someone?" Agent Archer asked.

I jumped and turned guiltily. "Just checking some things."

"In Keith's room?"

I pursed my lips. I had absolutely no response.

"I've checked all Keith's things. Fiona's, on the other hand? I can't check hers because I don't have a good enough reason or a warrant."

"Oh."

"She's in room four."

"Interesting."

Agent Archer nodded. "See you around."

Was he telling me to look in Fiona's room? It was so hard to read some people, and Agent Archer could keep a straight face. I went to room four and fiddled with the lock until it opened. Ms. Medley should get better locks. I pushed the door open and hurried inside. I didn't know what Fiona was doing while Keith baked, but I assumed she would stay near the diner and pace or something.

Fiona's room was as neat as it had been on the train. I looked around without touching anything, then gave up and pulled a pair of gloves from my pocket. I'd learned to keep some with me since I kept finding myself in these situations. I moved things around, careful to put them back where I'd found them.

It crossed my mind that Agent Archer said he was putting up cameras. That meant someone might see that I broke into the room. It was too late to do anything now. A small garbage can sat in the corner. I rifled through it. At the bottom was a bunch of cut-up pieces of cloudy plastic that might have been in a container at one point. There wasn't a label or anything to tell me what it was. I pulled the garbage bag out and found a roll of clean bags underneath. I put one in. Fiona would assume the maid came in.

I couldn't see anything else, so I left the room, locking it behind me. I felt funny walking around with a bag of garbage, and I didn't know what to do with it since people were in my apartment and the diner. The sheriff's office wasn't the place I wanted to be when Jett wasn't there, but I needed to go somewhere.

I opened the door to see Jane at her desk.

"Hi, Ivy. What brings you here?"

"Are any of the officers in?"

"No, but if you have an emergency, I can get ahold of someone. They're all out making their rounds."

A new desk sat against the wall, and a woman was typing. I hadn't met her, so I didn't know what she did. I was just glad Jett had people to work with now that the budget for the county allowed it.

"No, it's fine."

The door opened behind me, and I turned to see Deputy Ledford. Not my favorite person, but I didn't think he disliked me as much as he did when he first came here.

"Miss Clark. What do you want?" he said. Okay, maybe he still disliked me.

"I'm just wondering if anyone here knows what this thing I found is." I put my gloves back on and ignored it when Ledford sighed and raised his eyebrow. I pulled out the plastic pieces and held some of them in my hand.

Ledford studied the pieces, then shrugged. "I hope this isn't something the FBI is working on. I don't think they want your meddling."

"I think they might."

Ledford rubbed a finger over his mustache and shook his head. "You never cease to amaze me."

Jane came over and looked through her dark-rimmed glasses and into my hand. She was the secretary here but used to be a police officer. "It looks like the type of plastic they use to make the vanilla bottles I use."

"Imitation vanilla?" I asked. All the vanilla I'd ever had was in a glass bottle.

"Yep."

I smiled, then frowned. "Now what?" I said under my breath. If Fiona had the bottle someone used to switch Gavin's vanilla, she must be guilty of something.

"I'm assuming that's a clue you aren't supposed to have?" Ledford said.

"Probably. The FBI couldn't search the room I found it in, so now I'm not sure what to do."

Ledford rubbed a hand over his face, and I thought about reminding him of the time I saved him. He might not be here if I hadn't been trespassing that time. I shouldn't have said anything to him or even come here, but Jett was busy. If he hadn't come in, I would have shown Jane, and she wouldn't judge me. Well, she might, but I wouldn't know she was judging me because she was nice.

He sighed. "Take it to the agent and tell him where you got it. This isn't my case, and I don't want anything to do with it."

I nodded.

"Where's Sheriff Malone?" Jane asked.

"The contest today was only for one person and his name was drawn. He's probably in my apartment burning homemade pretzels."

Jane laughed. "I can't wait to watch this show."

"I hope I never see it," I said. "It's so awkward."

Ledford slipped past me and sat at his desk.

"I'll see you later," I told Jane.

There was still a little time before we were supposed to meet at the diner, so I took the bag of garbage back to the B&B and found Agent Archer sitting in a chair in the activity room.

"Hey," I said. "I decided to take Fiona's garbage out for her."

Agent Archer grinned. "That's nice of you."

"Yeah, there's a cut-up imitation vanilla bottle in the bottom."

He raised his brow. "Really? That seems really... careless."

"I agree. Why not put it in a different garbage?"

"Or maybe someone else put it there."

"I think some pieces are missing. She might have tried throwing it away in different places to make it unrecognizable."

"Hmm."

"I'm just going to leave it here," I said, putting it on the table. "I need to get back to the diner."

"Me too," he said, grabbing the garbage bag.

When I got to the diner, I sat in a booth and waited. Fiona was already there with her team. She wore a yellow dress with matching heels. I was only wearing jeans and a green shirt. Now that I was home, I felt silly putting on the fancy clothes I bought in Flagstaff. But after seeing Fiona, I was having second thoughts. I knew Jett didn't care what Fiona looked like, but I didn't want to look plain next to her.

I still had twenty minutes until we needed to be here, so I went up the stairs at the side of the dining area that led to my room. Before I'd had my place expanded, the room had been my only living area. I was glad I left these stairs because I could go into my room and change without bothering anyone by entering my apartment.

Once inside, I opened my closet and pulled out a knee-length black dress. I hadn't worn it yet because I knew it would draw attention, and I don't usually like people staring at me. I pulled it on before I could change my mind and grabbed some strappy black heels. My hair was a little windblown, so I ran my brush through it. My makeup still looked fine, so I opened my door and stood at the top of the stairs.

Being intimidated by Fiona was ridiculous. I took a breath and went down into the dining area. Jett, Boyd, and José were sitting in a booth. Keith sat by Fiona, and Colby had a table to himself. Agent Archer sat in the booth off in the corner where the cameras wouldn't be on him.

I could feel everyone in the room staring at me, and I regretted changing. If the looks on Colby, Keith, and Agent Archer's faces were any sign, I'd succeeded with my outfit. I didn't want to see the looks on my team's faces, so I walked over without looking at them. I sat next to Jett and glanced at Boyd, who was across from me.

"Is it almost time?"

"Theo is having someone bring in the trays, so you got here just in time," José said.

I nodded.

Jett took off his blue jacket. "Do you want to wear this?"

I tilted my head. "No, it's warm in here."

"But if you wear it, all the idiots in the room might stop staring at you."

I ducked my head. "I knew I shouldn't get this dress."

"No, you definitely should have, but you shouldn't wear it until Agent Archer is thousands of miles away."

Boyd chuckled, and José smiled.

"Not Colby and Keith?" Boyd asked.

José laughed quietly. "They aren't a threat."

"No one is," I said. "You guys are all crazy."

"You can all go back to what you were doing," Jett said loud enough for everyone to hear. Colby and Keith both turned back to their phones, and Agent Archer only smiled. I wanted to hide.

"Oh my heck, Jett," I said. "That was so embarrassing."

He sighed and put his arm around my shoulders. "Sorry. I've gotten weird ever since we started dating. I know I can't make you run around in an ugly cat apron just to get people to ignore you."

I smiled when I thought about the neon cat apron Jett had given me a long time ago. For my birthday, he cut it up and gave me two nice purple aprons.

"You were weird before you started dating," Boyd said.

José grinned. "Agreed."

"We've been dating for over four months now," Jett said, ignoring his friends. "I should be used to it."

I wrinkled my nose. "I think it's been one month."

"That's when we officially discussed it, but I'm counting from at least January."

I nodded. That made sense. January was the first time he kissed me.

A group of people brought trays with three plates to all three contestants. Theo and Bianca came in and signaled the cameras.

Theo turned to the room. "This contest will be judged differently. Each group will vote for the best food. You can try your teammate's food, but you can only vote for one of your competitors. One vote per team. All of you go ahead and try them. Bianca and I will also vote."

A camera came over near us, and I felt self-conscious. I looked down at Jett's pretzel. It was almost shaped like a pretzel and was slightly burned. The salt was falling off, and it was all uneven.

I smiled at Jett, and he shrugged. "For how much I messed up, you should be glad it looks that good."

Another plate had a flat cookie. Shortbread, maybe? The third was a crusty-looking brownie. The shortbread was good. Nothing too exciting, but I liked it. The brownie was almost impossible to eat. The pretzel was alright, but nothing I would eat on purpose.

"I think the shortbread wins," I said. "No contest."

"I agree," said José. "Even if we could vote for our own."

Jett grinned. "Thanks a lot."

"Yep. Definitely the shortbread," said Boyd.

"You guys were the ones who invited me. You knew my skills or lack thereof."

"What do you eat when you're home?" I asked. "You must cook sometimes."

"Sure. Anything that can cook in the microwave or comes from a can. Did you know you can get cookies already shaped in circles that you just pop in the oven? No preparation required."

"I didn't know about those until I moved in with Jett," Boyd said. "They aren't really good, though, so I would only get them if I was desperate."

When Theo announced today's winner, the shortbread was almost unanimous. We got one vote since no one was going to vote for the brownie.

"Yes!" Colby said, punching his hands in the air in victory. "Man, today was stressful."

Keith was looking at his phone, not concerned by his loss. Fiona was glaring at him, but he didn't seem to notice.

Chapter 15

I was surprised to find Jett and the puppy at my door early the following morning.

"What's going on?" I asked as they entered.

"I've come to show you that this dog is not going to get along with Creepers," Jett said, sitting on the living room floor. He put the puppy down, and it chewed on his shoelaces.

I shook my head, and my ponytail slapped me in the face. "You don't have to keep the puppy. I shouldn't have taken him."

"I have to keep him. Boyd's in love. Where's Creepers?"

"I'm not sure. Let me look." I went to my room and found him curled up on my bed. He yawned and glanced at me. I scooped him up and carried him into the living room.

Creepers looked down at the puppy, then up at me.

My mouth turned down. "I'm afraid to put him down."

"Sit with him so they can look at each other."

I sat cross-legged and kept ahold of Creepers. The puppy came curiously over and sniffed at the cat. Creepers froze. He was bigger than the puppy but unsure what to do. My heart was pounding as I waited for one of them to swipe at the other.

Creepers stepped over my leg and rubbed his head against the puppy.

"What's he doing?" I whispered.

"I think Creepers likes him."

"No way."

The puppy licked Creeper's face, and the cat took a few steps back, still staring.

"What do you think?" Jett asked.

"I don't know. I thought Creepers would run or scratch."

"Come on, let's sit on the couch and see what they do."

We moved onto the couch, and the puppy went closer to Creepers. Creepers sat down, and the puppy curled up next to him.

"You can't tell me that wasn't the cutest thing you've ever seen," I said. "It looks like a picture from a calendar."

Jett put his arm around me. "It is pretty cute. I was sure it would be a disaster. We'll have to put them together at least a few times a week so they keep liking each other."

I rested my head against Jett and watched the two animals snuggle. I never would have believed Creepers would like a dog, especially the first time he met it. He hadn't been around any, so he probably didn't even know what a dog was.

"Have you named him?" I asked.

"No. He's staying with Brian until the contest is over. I'm thinking something like Conan or He-Man."

I looked up at him. "Seriously? He's too cute for those names."

"Boyd's already calling him Conan."

The door opened, and my parents walked in. I blinked. "Mom? Dad? What are you doing here?"

My mom laughed. "We thought we would surprise you."

"Well, I'm surprised." I stood and hugged my mom. "It feels like it's been a long time." I turned and hugged my dad.

"Hello, Sheriff," my mom said, shaking Jett's hand when he stood.

"It's good to see you again, Mrs. Clark."

"You too. This is my husband, Hank. Hank, this is Sheriff Malone."

Jett shook my dad's hand. "Nice to meet you. You can call me Jett."

"I should hope so if you're hugging my daughter."

My eyes went wide. How had I not registered that Jett's arm had been around me when they walked in?

My mom elbowed him in the stomach, and Jett cleared his throat nervously.

"You got a dog?" my mom asked, dropping to her knees. "How adorable! And Creepers likes him."

"It's Jett's dog. Sort of," I said.

"Sort of?" my mom asked, rubbing the puppy's head.

"I'm taking him after the competition," Jett said.

"What competition?"

"You didn't tell your parents about the competition?" Jett asked.

"It seems you haven't told us about a lot of things," my mom said, looking up and winking at me.

"I've been really busy. Sorry."

"What's the dog's name?"

"Conan," Jett said, grinning at me.

I cringed. "That's a horrible name."

"I like it." My dad nodded.

I shook my head.

"So what's this competition?" my mom asked.

I gave her a quick overview, leaving out Gavin and the murder.

"I can't believe you didn't mention it. It sounds exciting! I can't wait to watch it."

I shrugged. "It's not a big deal. Just a YouTube channel. I'm not going to watch it."

"Why not?"

"It's awkward."

"Do you need to get to the diner?"

"No, I have people coming in this morning. You haven't seen my apartment! You should look around."

"I've been dying to see it," my mom said, walking to the kitchen. "It's adorable! I love it," she said loudly. My dad followed her in.

"Can I leave?" Jett whispered. "Your dad is giving me the look."

I smiled. "My dad isn't scary. Don't worry."

They came back out and went down the hall to look at the guest room.

"I bet they'll want to stay," I said. "That will be weird with the show."

They came back out, and my dad sat on the couch. He patted the spot next to him. "Sit, Jett."

I frowned. "Dad—"

"It's alright," Jett said, sitting next to him.

My dad turned to him. "So, Jett. What are your intentions with my daughter?"

"Oh my heck, Dad," I muttered. My mom laughed softly.

Jett rubbed his chin. "It depends. Do you mean short-term or long-term? I mean, we might as well get it all out now and not ever have to do this again. We've been dating for a while, and we're planning on the long haul."

My mom sank down into the recliner and looked at me. "And you haven't said anything?"

I shrugged. "Sorry. I've been busy, and it seemed weird to tell you on the phone."

"I can't believe no one has called and told me. I thought I was still in the Muddy Creek gossip circle. When did all this happen?"

"We've only been dating for a month," I said.

"Four months," Jett said.

"I thought I sensed something between you when I first met the sheriff."

The door opened, and Boyd came in.

"You should consider locking your door," Jett suggested.

Boyd chuckled. "I have a key so I can keep Creeper's company. Candy, good to see you!"

My mom stood and hugged Boyd. She'd grown up here, so she knew almost everyone.

"So have you been dating for a month or four months?" my dad asked. "That seems like a big discrepancy."

"They've been hooked at the lips for at least four months and wishing they were since Ivy drove into town almost a year ago," Boyd said.

"Don't you mean hooked at the hip?" my dad asked.

Boyd smiled. "I know what I've seen."

My face felt like fire, and I put my hands to my burning cheeks. "Boyd!"

160

"He's not wrong," Jett said, wrapping his arm around me.

My dad laughed and patted Jett on the shoulder.

"Boyd's crazy," I said. "He doesn't know how much—ugh."

Boyd laughed. "Candy already knows I'm crazy. Still, if I've spotted you kissing, what, three or four times? Then I figure it's happened way more than that."

"Did you need something?" I asked Boyd.

"I just came to play with Creepers. I thought you would be in the diner. It looks like he's getting along well with Conan."

I sighed. "I guess he's stuck as Conan." Talking about anything besides Jett and me was preferable.

Jett's phone pinged, and he pulled it from his pocket. "It's my mom. She's eating breakfast in the diner and wants me to meet her and bring you if you're free. You've got to be kidding."

"I haven't seen Carol in years," my mom said. "Let's all go down and have breakfast together."

"You know Carol?" I asked.

"Of course."

I looked at Jett. I couldn't think of an escape.

"I'll watch the animals," Boyd offered. "I think I'll sit on the couch, though, so I don't get stuck on the floor."

Jett grabbed my hand, and we followed my parents through my room and down the stairs into the diner. Carol stood when she saw us.

"Candy! It's been years!" She rushed over and hugged my mom. This was so weird. I'd never thought about our moms knowing each other.

We sat awkwardly at one of the bigger tables while our moms caught up. Livy came by and took our orders. The diner was filling up with people from the show. I was glad to see my parents, but I wished they hadn't come until the show was over. Now I might be distracted.

"Did you know I was Candy's 4-H leader?" Carol asked Jett.

"Nope," Jett said, sipping his water.

"Who would have thought our kids would end up dating?" Carol said to Candy.

"We only just found out!" Candy said. "I can't believe no one told us."

"You didn't tell Ivy's parents?" Carol gave Jett an annoyed look. "That doesn't seem fair. I've known for weeks."

My mom raised her eyebrow and looked at me.

"Hey," Jett said. "To be fair, none of you would know if any of you knocked."

Carol laughed. "Maybe you should lock your doors."

Jett grinned. "You came into my house with a key, Ma."

"Fair enough. Well, I, for one, am thrilled. We think Ivy is wonderful. She's making quite the name for herself in this town."

"Because of the diner?" my mom asked.

"Well, that and all the mysteries she's solved."

My parents both looked at me.

"Mysteries, as in plural?" my mom asked.

Carol nodded. "They sure seem to follow her, don't they? I told Jett he should convince her to go to the academy so she can become his deputy. The deputy he has now is hard to swallow."

I stopped listening to Carol's description of Ledford. I could feel my mom's eyes on me. I'd always loved mysteries, and my mom had worried when I was young. She'd even convinced my Gramma Sue to put a provision in her will that said she would pay for my education so long as it didn't involve law enforcement or anything like it.

Our food came, and I tried to think of a way to change the flow of the conversation. I was glad Jett's mom didn't know all the things I'd done to solve a crime because she was telling my parents everything she knew. I hadn't advertised the dangerous parts, and it appeared Jett hadn't either. I told myself I was thirty and didn't have to follow someone else's path for me, but I still didn't want to worry my mom.

I ate quickly, and so did Jett. Neither one of us was contributing to the conversation.

"Do you love Jett's puppy?" my mom asked Carol. "It's so cute."

Carol turned to Jett. "You got a puppy? How come you never tell me anything anymore?"

"I didn't exactly get a puppy," Jett said, bumping me with his shoulder. "Ivy took a puppy that Brian couldn't keep and brought it to me. Boyd fell in love with it in about two seconds, and now I'm stuck."

"Stuck?" his mom asked. "You love dogs."

"It's a Maltese. It's basically a cat that barks."

"But Creepers likes him," I said.

Jett tilted his head and looked at me. "They've only seen each other once, so I don't know if that will last. You know what other problem it's going to cause?"

"What?"

"Boyd. He already loves that thing. What's he going to do when I move out? He'll be all alone."

I bit the inside of my cheek while I thought. I didn't want Boyd to go back to being lonely again. He'd ridden his bike into town every day when he lived on his own so he could be with people. Now he had Jett, so he had someone to talk to at night.

"I have a spare room—"

"Nooooo," Jett said. "I love Boyd, but your apartment is small, and I don't want to live that close to Boyd. My house is big so we aren't tripping over each other."

I rubbed my lips together and looked at the ceiling. "Hmm. You could leave the dog with Boyd."

"He can't take care of it by himself."

"Well, we can't leave Boyd all alone." I looked across at my mom and noticed she had an enormous grin on her face. It was almost as big as Carol's. I'd almost forgotten they were there.

"We can figure it out later," Jett said.

"Are we talking about getting married?" Carol asked.

Jett chuckled. "I think we're talking about Boyd."

"It sounds like the two of you have become his parents," my dad said.

"I feel like he's my grandpa," I said. "I don't know how I made it through life before I came to Muddy Creek."

"Because of Boyd?" Jett asked, grinning.

I smiled. "Among other things."

"Why would you move out of your house?" Carol asked Jett.

Jett rolled his eyes. "Come on, Ma. I'm not telling you all of my secrets. Besides, we were talking about the future, not today."

All three of the parents were staring at us. I looked up at Jett. "Don't we have somewhere to be?" I joked.

"I'm still technically on vacation, and we don't start the show until tonight."

"Just tell us your future plans, and we'll leave you alone," Carol said.

My mom nodded. "We aren't prying. We're just being moms."

"It sounds like their plans are to get hitched and take care of a puppy and Boyd," my dad said.

I got distracted by something out of the corner of my eye. I saw someone disappear behind the wall, which meant they were going up the stairs to my room. Kids occasionally wandered over there, but there weren't any kids today.

I leaned toward Jett. "I think someone is going up the stairs to my room." I started to stand, but Jett grabbed my arm and pulled me back.

"Let me go." He got up and walked quietly over. He looked around the wall and frowned. "That's not part of the diner," he said.

Fiona came from around the corner. "Sorry, I thought the bathroom was over here."

"Nope," Jett said, pointing at the big sign on the other side of the room that said "Restrooms."

Fiona smiled and walked in that direction.

Jett sat back down and looked at me, frowning. "Fiona has been using the restroom in here for days. She's up to something."

"She can't get into my room from here. That lock you put on was too strong to pick, especially by Fiona."

"Probably, but be careful."

I nodded, and my mom frowned.

Chapter 16

Theo announced that tonight was the last night of the competition. It was supposed to have a few more rounds, but because so many things had gone bad, they were making tonight the finale. I was relieved, but I wondered if there would be time to get to the bottom of Gavin's murder. Keith was still at the top of my list, but now I wondered if Fiona was involved as well.

The final contest was to make a dinner and dessert. José was busy cutting up chicken, and he had Boyd peeling potatoes. Jett was frying bacon, and I was making éclairs. It was nice not to see the other teams, but at the same time annoying that I couldn't see what they were doing.

"You alright, Ivs?" Jett asked.

"Yeah, just thinking."

"About our parents?"

"No. I'm wondering what Keith is doing."

"Ten bucks says he's playing *Fruit Ninja* on his phone," José said.

"I'm more worried about our parents," Jett said. "You know they're going to be hanging out for hours? By the time we see them again, they'll probably have named all our future children."

I laughed. "I can see my mom doing that. Not my dad."

One of the camera operators flipped on his camera, and we all went quiet. I needed to concentrate anyway if I wanted to get the filling right. Éclairs aren't the hardest thing, but if you aren't careful, they can be ugly and leak everywhere.

"Are people yelling downstairs?" Boyd asked.

I stopped and listened. "I think so." My brows knit together. I wanted to run down and see what was happening, but I doubted Theo would appreciate that.

"It's happening out back," said one of the camera crew.

I went to the window and looked out. Theo, Fiona, and Agent Archer were all outside, and Fiona was yelling about something and pointing at Theo. She charged at Theo, but Agent Archer grabbed her around the waist and pulled her back.

"Fiona tried to attack Theo," I said. "Agent Archer is holding her back."

"I better go," Jett said, rushing from the kitchen.

Fiona tried to claw at Agent Archer, but he held her out of reach. Her neat updo had come loose, and her hair hung in her face. I opened the window to see if I could hear anything.

"Keith!" Fiona bellowed. "Keith, help me!"

Jett descended the stairs and said something to Agent Archer that I couldn't hear. Keith came out the back door and stood with his hands in his pockets.

"Do something, Keith!" Fiona yelled.

Keith just stood there watching and shrugged his shoulders. If he said something, I didn't catch it.

"Stop!" Agent Archer commanded when Fiona tried to bite him.

"Run, Keith!" she demanded.

Keith didn't run, and I still couldn't hear. I left the kitchen and the apartment and went down the stairs.

"What's going on?" Keith was saying.

"Just run!" Fiona said. "I'm doing this for you."

"What are you talking about?"

Agent Archer twisted Fiona around and pulled her arms behind her back. She was struggling hard, so Jett came up next to them and handcuffed her.

"What did she do?" Keith asked.

"Tampered with evidence and tried to drug an agent," said Agent Archer.

Keith's eyes narrowed. "Mom?"

"Don't give me that!" Fiona growled. "Don't look concerned and confused. I did this for you!"

Deputy Ledford came around the building. "I heard there was a disturbance?"

"Yes," Agent Archer said. "Can you lock this woman up until I'm ready to deal with her?"

"Of course," Ledford said, taking Fiona's arm. Ledford might be short, but he was strong. He pulled Fiona with him and quickly disappeared from the way he came.

"Don't give up!" Fiona yelled. I assumed to Keith.

"Sorry about that," Keith said. "My mom's a bit high-strung sometimes. She tried to drug someone?"

Theo nodded. "I saw her put some sleeping pills into some tea this morning. I thought it was for her, but she tried to give it to Agent Archer."

"Why would she do that?" Keith asked.

"To protect you is my guess," Agent Archer said. "I think she was listening when I got a phone call before we started filming. Vonna admitted to having you swap out Gavin's vanilla. When I left the room after the call, Fiona was standing near the door glaring at me."

Keith looked at his feet. "Yeah, I switched the vanilla for Vonna. She told me it didn't matter because she was part of the show and could bring ingredients."

"She said she believes you were the one to kill Gavin."

"I didn't kill Gavin," Keith said. "Why would I do that?"

"Because Vonna was paying attention to you, and you knew she was targeting him for whatever reason."

"She wanted to stir something up, but nothing like that. I don't even care about this stupid competition. That's all my mom."

Agent Archer's eyebrow rose. "Well, your mom seems to think she needs to protect you from something."

"She's always like that. She thinks I'm getting into trouble all the time. Go to jail once, and no one trusts you anymore."

"I'm going to have to ask you some more questions," Agent Archer said. "If Vonna and your mom think you were behind it, I need to look into it."

"I don't know anything about the berries from Gavin's pie. There's no way I ever would have thought to do something like that."

"Well, come talk to me inside." The two of them disappeared back into the diner.

"This season is a mess," Theo said, running a hand through his gray and black hair. "I couldn't have planned it better if I tried. Our ratings are going to be great."

"Someone died," Jett said. "You think that's a good thing?"

"For ratings, it is."

I narrowed my eyes and studied Theo. He didn't look like the type to cause this type of drama, but it was his show and money riding on this season.

"Are we still baking?" I asked.

"Yes," Theo said. "There are still two members from Calico Café and that's one more than The Velvet Pearl has."

"Is it fair that we still have four?"

"Fair has nothing to do with it," Theo said. "Those teams lost people because of their own bad choices. You should probably get baking. Time is ticking."

Jett and I went back upstairs and stopped in the living room.

"Could Theo be behind it?" I whispered so none of the crew could hear.

"It's possible," Jett murmured. "I'll talk to Agent Archer after he's done with Keith."

"I'm surprised they haven't made us cancel the entire competition."

"They probably should have. Clear back when Gavin died."

We went back and finished baking. By the time we were finished, it was time to take everything down to the diner. Colby was the only one in the kitchen.

"Where is everyone?" José asked.

Colby shrugged. "I don't know what's going on. I think Keith was arrested, and the rest of their team left. This contest is a joke. I bet no network picks it up and no one watches it. Even though there have been a lot of crazy things happening, the rest of the contest has been boring. Theo doesn't know how to carry a show."

"What?" Theo asked, walking into the room.

"Nothing," Colby muttered.

"That's what I thought. Get into the dining room so we can taste everything."

We all went and sat down. Bianca and Theo sat and waited for someone to bring them the platters of food. Colby had made a pasta dish, and our group had a chicken, potato, and bacon casserole. The judges tasted both. Neither one of them looked like they wanted to be here. Bianca appeared tired, but her eyes lit up when she tasted José's creation.

"That's the best thing I've had since the show began," she said.

Theo nodded. "It's good. The Velvet Pearl's pasta is too dry."

Colby sighed.

"The desserts are both nice," he said. "Sue's Diner wins. Not that it was a great competition this year."

José smiled, but I was just glad to be finished. I couldn't believe that was the way they announced it. Nothing exciting. José said people tried to get into this show, which was competitive, but I didn't see a wow factor in how they did this.

"Clean up," Theo said. "The sooner we get out of this place, the better. This season will be great, but I am so done."

I looked at Jett, and he shrugged.

Everyone cleared out, and Agent Archer came back to talk to Jett. I went up to my apartment and grabbed Creepers. I sat on the recliner and petted him absentmindedly. Boyd had taken the puppy back to Brian before the competition. Creepers was looking around, and I wondered if he missed his new friend.

There was a knock on my door, and my mom came in.

"Hey, Mom. Where's Dad?"

"He's with Tanner Malone. Last I saw them, they were playing Ping-Pong."

I smiled when I tried to picture my dad with Jett's dad, playing Ping-Pong.

"I've been talking to people around town today," she said. "They've all been telling me about your adventures. I thought you had decided not to follow a career in crime?"

"It's not a career. It just happens."

"You've solved several murders! When I call and ask what you're up to, you always say something like not much. Ivy, this is dangerous."

"It's fine."

She raised her brow. "Someone told me you were locked in a bathroom once, and Jett was tied up! That's not fine."

"I don't know what to tell you. I've always been interested in this type of thing. That's why you decided I couldn't have a career in crime. I didn't decide that."

She sighed. "I hope you're careful."

"Don't worry. I'm fine."

"Well, tell me about Jett. How did that all happen? He seems like a nice man."

"He is."

"I thought you might be interested in him the last time I was here. His parents are wonderful people. I've known Carol my entire life. It sounds like the two of you are serious?"

"Yes."

"That was fast."

"It doesn't feel like it. I've liked him since I moved here."

"He makes you happy?"

"Every day."

"I'm glad. I've always wanted good things for you."

I smiled. "Muddy Creek has been good for me. The people here are great, and I love the diner. Did you notice Gramma Sue's jukebox works again?"

"I did. I used to love that thing."

"José fixed it. I think he regrets it. Boyd has a lot of nickels, and he only plays the same three songs every day."

My mom grinned. "That sounds like Boyd. I'm glad you've taken an interest in him. It must be lonely to be all alone at his age."

"He's been great for me. He's one of the funniest guys I know." I couldn't share many examples because a lot of them happened while I was solving cases, and I didn't think I should go back to that topic. She wouldn't appreciate knowing that Boyd had also helped solve all the murders.

"So your contest is over?"

"Yes."

"Did you win?"

"Yeah, but half the people we were competing against were gone at the end, so it doesn't feel like a rewarding win."

"I always knew your baking would be famous someday."

I laughed. "It's not famous. I'm glad José will get some recognition. He's really the talented one, and he deserves it."

Chapter 17

The town book club met in the diner once a week. I thought Barbra ran it, but she might just be the person who talked the most. We had a small party room, and they reserved it and talked and ate cookies. I placed the cookies on the table and began to leave.

"Why don't you ever join us, Ivy?" Barbra asked. "It's a lot of fun."

I turned. "Maybe next time. What are you reading?"

"*Gone With the Wind.*"

"I bet Boyd loved that," I teased.

"I'm guessing not since he didn't show up," Opal said, snatching a cookie.

"Have you read it?" Barbra asked.

"In high school."

"Did you enjoy it?"

"Some of it. I thought it was hard to relate to because I didn't like the characters. It's hard to feel sympathetic to someone as selfish as the people in there."

"Exactly what I was just saying!" Opal said. "Why don't we read something with likable characters? We keep reading books with no redeeming traits."

"Read a mystery," I suggested.

Opal shook her head. "I've had enough mystery in my life. If I wanted a mystery, I would go look around Barbra's attic."

Barbra pushed her purple hair back. "My attic isn't a mystery. It's a mess. And it's not even my mess."

I tilted my head. "What do you mean?"

"I bought that house as is about a hundred years ago." Everyone laughed at her exaggeration. "My husband and I spent weeks throwing stuff out. By the time we cleaned out the main house, we didn't want to deal with the attic, so who knows what's in there."

"I can't believe you didn't tell me!" I said. "That would be fun to go through."

"That's why I didn't tell you," she said. "You've already been decluttering my house. I didn't want you volunteering to do the attic as well."

"But I would love to!" I said, feeling excited. "How long ago did you really move there?"

"About forty years ago."

"We're already planning on selling a bunch of the stuff we've found in your house. We might as well look in the attic and see if anything is valuable." A lot of Barbra's stuff had been donated, but we kept things we thought might sell and were waiting until we finished cleaning out the entire house.

"Now look what you've done," Barbra told Opal. "Now Ivy's going to spend even more of her valuable time cleaning up my junk."

"Someone needs to."

"I suppose."

"We still have a few more rooms in the main part of the house to go." Barbra had so much stuff. She'd kept pretty much everything she'd come across in the past thirty years.

I smiled. "I'm happy to help, and you know I love to snoop. Think of the exciting things that might be in the attic. I can't believe you've never looked."

"I poked around a bit, but it's been untouched so long it would probably give a person asthma. Think of all the bugs and dust."

"I'm up for it."

Barbra laughed. "I'm sure you are. Maybe I'll leave my attic to you in my will. You can keep all the garbage from the people before me. I've stuffed things up there as well. It's probably a fire hazard."

"I'll leave you to your book and talk to you about it later," I said. I left and went into the dining area. My mind wasn't going to settle until I saw Barbra's attic.

"Hi, Colby," I said when I spotted him at a booth. He was sitting in front of a pile of pancakes.

"Hey. Congratulations on your win. You guys deserved it."

"Thanks. I'm surprised you're still here."

He shrugged. "Theo said we can all stay for another two nights. Muddy Creek isn't my dream vacation, but I'll take what I can get."

"Is anyone else still here?"

"Yeah. Theo and Bianca are still here, and I saw one of the crew members I don't know. I think everyone else is staying in Wichita."

"Where are Theo and Bianca?"

"Sitting in the hot tub at the B&B. I would be there too, but I've had enough of them."

"I guess I wasn't around them enough to get sick of them," I said. "What are your plans once you get home?"

"My boss said I can have a paid week off to recover from everything. He's a good guy."

"That's nice of him."

"Yeah. He's stressed about Gavin, but he's holding it together. Did you hear Keith was being interrogated?"

"Yes."

"I guess he admitted to changing out Gavin's vanilla, but he only admitted it because he felt they had enough evidence. He said he didn't kill Gavin, but that could just be because they haven't found evidence."

I nodded. "Do you mind if I sit with you?"

"Go for it."

I sat and waved Livy over. "Can you bring me a hot chocolate?"

"Sure," Livy said, rushing away.

"Hot chocolate? It seems warm for that," Colby said.

"It is. I have a problem. I love hot chocolate. Sometimes I purposely make myself cold so I can have it."

He laughed.

"I thought after the way Theo reacted at the end of the show, he would be long gone."

"So did I. The B&B is pretty nice, though. It has a nice pool and hot tub. I think I'll spend today in the pool. It's been a while since I could just relax. I heard around town that you teach a Zumba class."

"Yes. It's been a couple of weeks, but I should start again tomorrow if you're bored."

He laughed. "I think I'll pass. I heard it's mostly old ladies."

"And Boyd."

"That might make it worth it. I'm not coordinated, though, so I still think I'll pass."

"It doesn't take a lot of coordination. Getting people moving is my goal. It doesn't matter how they do it, just so they move."

The door opened, and Jett walked in. He ran a hand through his already messy hair and yawned. He was wearing his sheriff's uniform again. I frowned. That meant his vacation was over.

"The sheriff looks beat," Colby said.

"Yeah, I wonder why."

Jett came and sat next to me. "Hello. I'm surprised to see you around, Colby."

"I'll be here a few more days."

Jett turned to me. "Guess who doesn't sleep at night?"

"Who?"

"Conan. I don't know if he slept at all, and he whines if he's alone. Boyd fell asleep with his door closed, of course, and I'm guessing he took his hearing aids out because he was bright and chipper this morning. I slept with that little fluff ball on my face."

I tried to look sympathetic, but I'm sure my eyes were shining. "That's too bad."

"You owe me."

I smiled. "You wanted a dog."

"Yeah, yeah. Not right now. I'm going to let him in Boyd's room tonight. Or maybe I'll slip him in your place."

"We heard Keith was with the police or something?"

"I don't know exactly what happened," he said. "I do know Agent Archer took both Keith and Fiona with him when he left town last night."

"I feel bad for Keith," Colby said. "I bet he didn't mean to kill Gavin. It's sad, really."

"So Agent Archer is finished here?" I asked.

"As far as I know. Is anyone else from the show still here?"

"Theo and Bianca at least," I said.

"Weird. I thought they would be gone the fastest."

"Nope," Colby said. "They're hogging the hot tub at the B&B. I guess I could go in with them, but that seems weird. I'm actually hoping I never have to talk to either of them again. I doubt I'll even watch the show."

Boyd came walking into the diner holding Conan.

"You can't bring a dog in here," I said, jumping up.

"I'll take him up to see Creepers."

I followed him back out and up to my apartment. I unlocked the door and let him in. Creepers jumped off the couch and wandered over to Boyd. He put the puppy down, and Creepers rubbed against Conan.

"I still can't believe they like each other," I said.

"Yeah, but you better not get too attached. I heard Jett and Conan all night last night. Jett was grumbling all morning about him."

"He won't get rid of him. He's complaining, but I can tell he likes him."

"Yeah. I told him Conan needs to learn to sleep on his own, but as soon as he whined, Jett let him in the bed. It's going to be a spoiled dog. I should probably let Conan sleep in my room. I can ignore things like dogs crawling over me, and I can sleep in if I want to."

"Jett looked tired today."

"Was that Colby I saw in there? I thought everyone would have cleared out."

"Yeah. A few people are staying for a while."

"You don't think Keith did it, do you?"

I smiled. "What do you mean?"

"You look distracted. Like you're still trying to figure something out."

"I've thought Keith was guilty the entire time. I just wonder about Fiona. I think she suspected Keith did it, and that was why she snuck into Gavin's room. She was looking for anything that might point at him. The vanilla bottle was cut up in her garbage can. I bet she found it and didn't want Keith to get in trouble for it. He was already on probation, so this would make it a lot worse."

"So you do think it was Keith?"

"Probably. It's hard to say."

"I'm going to stay here with these two and let them get to know each other better. You don't have to stay for me."

I nodded. "Let me know if you need anything."

I went downstairs and sat down. My hot chocolate was waiting for me. Colby was almost finished eating, and Jett was off in the corner on the phone.

"Boyd's an interesting character," Colby said.

"He's fun."

Jett came back to the table. "That was Agent Archer. The toxicology report came in."

Colby's phone rang. "Excuse me," he said. "I have to take this." He stood and walked a few feet away.

"Did the report say anything interesting?"

"They found that the berries and the cashew shells together are what killed him. Agent Archer seemed surprised about the cashews."

"But we already knew about them."

"Agent Archer said he didn't."

"Then how did we?" My heart began pounding. "Colby told me about them." I turned to ask Colby who had told him, but he was gone.

Chapter 18

I ran out of the diner and looked both ways down the street. Jett was right behind me.

"Don't go after him," he said. "I'll look."

"Could he have done it?" I said. "Why would he tell us about the cashews if he did it? That would make him look completely guilty."

"He might have figured people already knew."

"Someone might have told him. I don't want to think it was Colby. He didn't seem to have anything too bad against Gavin."

"What if he wanted the attention on him?" Jett said.

"But he didn't give off that vibe. Besides, we figure whoever did it was probably targeting the judges—Wait." I closed my eyes and tried to remember a conversation I'd had with Colby.

"Are you okay?"

I looked at Jett and frowned. "When Gavin ate the pie, Colby said Gavin had done something similar before with an over-seasoned chicken. I bet Colby assumed the judges would criticize it, and Gavin would eat the pie to try to show them it wasn't as bad as they thought."

"I should call Agent Archer."

"But what if someone else told Colby about the cashews?"

Jett rubbed the back of his neck. "It's possible."

"I bet whatever was in the bag Vonna threw off the train was the remnants of the crushed cashews."

"Yeah, Agent Archer said it was."

"But Vonna had that, not Colby."

"Maybe Vonna told Colby about the shells?"

"We need to find him. If he ran off, that makes him look guilty."

Jett nodded. "Yeah, but he was finished eating, and he was on the phone. He might have just been ready to go. I'll go look at the B&B. Is there anywhere else he might go?"

"Not that I know of."

"You stay in the diner."

"I'm going to go check on Creepers, then I will."

Jett nodded and jogged off down the street. I went around the back of the diner and paused when I saw Colby sitting on the steps going up to my apartment. He was still on the phone. I quickly texted Jett and told him.

Colby put his phone in his pocket and smiled slightly when he saw me.

"Are you alright?" I asked.

"Fine," he said.

"Hey, who told you about the crushed-up cashew shells when we were on the train?"

He frowned. "Umm... I think it was Vonna."

I nodded. That would make sense since she had the baggie.

He shifted nervously. I'd been ready to believe him, but now I wasn't sure. He looked guilty. Jett would come running around the corner any moment.

"Vonna wouldn't have expected Gavin to eat the pie. If it was her, she was aiming at the judges."

"I thought it was Keith?"

"I think Keith looks guilty because he switched the vanilla. That might have been his only crime."

Colby ran a hand over his goatee. "Hmm. So it was Vonna? I never would have thought."

"I don't think it was. I think it was you."

Colby barked out a laugh. "Me? Why would I kill Gavin?"

"Maybe it was an accident. You just wanted to make him sick, perhaps? You knew he would eat the pie when the judges criticized it. Just like he ate the over-seasoned chicken."

"Everyone knew he would eat it. He did it with the pinwheel."

"True, but you knew him better than everyone. I think you sabotaged it and also messed with our sugar. That made it look like Fiona's team was behind it all. Then you hid the baggie of ground shells in Vonna's bag, and she freaked out and tried to get rid of it."

He stared at me for a moment. "Come on, Ivy," he said. "You know that doesn't make any sense. Why would I do that?"

"Because Gavin was a jerk, and you were sick of him. No one knew about the cashew shells. Agent Archer only found out about them today. You knew a long time ago."

Colby sighed. "Gavin was a jerk. You're right about that. He took credit for everything and thought he was the only one who knew anything. I didn't mean to kill him. I just wanted to make him suffer and miss the train. You can understand that, right?"

"I can understand being annoyed at someone, but you crossed lines."

"I'll just leave and never bother you again."

I walked closer. "You can't leave. You killed Gavin."

"Don't make me hurt you," he said, stepping back.

I stopped. "You can't get away. People are out looking for you." I didn't tell him it was only Jett. I took in his size. He wasn't much taller than me, and I doubted he had a weapon.

"You told them, didn't you? I thought we were going to be friends."

"Just turn yourself in. Tell them it was an accident."

"I'll still go to jail."

"You should."

He rolled his eyes. "Is this how you convince people? Look, I didn't mean to kill Gavin. I might have secretly hoped he would die, but I didn't think he would. No one cares. He didn't have people who liked him. My boss didn't even like him. He just kept him around because he was good. No one else had a chance to shine because everything even remotely complicated was given to Gavin."

"So you were jealous?"

"I'm not jealous!" he said. "It wasn't fair. He didn't deserve to have every opportunity. In any other place, he would have been fired for mouthing off at customers, but my boss liked that he won awards and got good reviews from critics."

He sounded jealous to me, but I didn't want to point it out. Where was Jett? He should have been right behind me. He must not have noticed my text.

"You need to turn yourself in. You can't get away. This town is small, and you don't have a car."

"Give me your keys," he said.

"I don't have my keys."

"Sure you do," he said, stepping toward me.

"I don't carry my car key around. I walk almost everywhere."

Yelling was an option. I could probably get José out here, but my parents were staying in my apartment, and I didn't want them coming into danger. I had a small bottle of pepper spray in my pocket that I had learned to keep with me. I'd never used it, but I would if I had to.

"Give me your keys. I know you have them."

I pulled the key to my apartment out and tossed it to him. He caught it and ran off, disappearing around the diner. He was going to be disappointed when he realized he couldn't open the car with them. I followed after him at a walk.

When I rounded the corner, it was to find Colby being held against the wall by Jett. He was reading Colby his rights. He cuffed him and yanked him away from the wall. My key was on the ground, so I picked it up.

"I expected you to have tackled him by now," Jett said, winking at me.

I smiled. "I wasn't feeling it today." Honestly, Colby was the first person I'd liked who had committed a crime, and I felt down about it. I didn't know him well, but it bothered me I'd been so convinced it was Keith.

I watched Jett and Colby walk toward the sheriff's office. Colby wasn't even putting up a fight. I went up to my apartment and found my parents on the couch watching a movie with Creepers curled up on my mom's lap. They didn't need me, so I went back down to the diner to check on the book club.

"Everyone okay in here?" I asked.

"Perfect," Barbra said. "We're really glad you added this room to the diner. It's so cozy."

"It is," I agreed. "Let me know if you need anything, alright?"

They all nodded, and I went to the kitchen. José was making a hamburger.

"You're alone today?"

José nodded. "I let the others have off. They've been working a lot."

"Jett just arrested Colby."

José turned. "What?"

"I was so wrong when I blamed Keith. He did the vanilla thing, but Colby killed Gavin."

"He confessed?"

"Yep."

"On his own?"

"After I confronted him. Agent Archer called and told Jett about the cashew shells. It was just discovered in the toxicology report, but Colby had told us before. He was the only one who knew."

"That was careless of him."

"Yeah, but it's good he did, or we might not have ever known it was him. I feel like I really failed this time."

José put the burger on a plate and put it out the window for Livy to pick up. "How are you a failure?"

"I felt sure it was Keith. I knew it could be anyone, but I focused on him. I barely had Colby on my radar. To me, he was just a nice guy. I was completely wrong."

"But in the end, you figured it out. Don't be hard on yourself."

"What are you going to do with the money from the competition?"

"What do you mean? We all get the money."

"We won because of you."

"It was all of us."

I smiled. "Yeah, but mostly you."

"We'll all take a share. I'll just sink mine into my house. That thing is falling apart. What about you?"

I shrugged. "I don't need anything right now."

"You might have to pay to fix everything that little puppy destroys at Jett's place. Boyd said he's already chewed up a kitchen chair and a rug since they took him yesterday."

"Oh no. I'm too compulsive. The dog was cute, and I acted too fast."

"A dog will be good for Boyd and probably Jett. All puppies destroy things. It will get easier."

Chapter 19

"So what happened?" Boyd asked from his seat at my small kitchen table.

Jett put down his glass of water. "Everyone confessed. Agent Archer said that once everyone knew Colby was guilty, they all confessed to what they'd done."

"Makes sense," José said. "They were all worried they looked guilty of the murder, so what they did was mellow in comparison."

"Yep," Jett said. "Vonna got Keith to switch the vanilla, and Fiona found out. She freaked and started snooping in everyone's rooms to try to find any evidence that would point to Keith. She found the imitation vanilla bottle in Keith's things and cut the bottle up and tried to slowly dispose of it. When Gavin was killed, she thought it was Keith, so she got even stranger. Vonna also thought Keith did it, so she worried she would look guilty because she had him switch the vanilla. It happened just like Ivy guessed."

"And Colby confessed?" Boyd asked.

Jett nodded. "Yes. He's saying he didn't mean to kill him. I don't know what will happen. It's the FBI's case, so I'm not sure how it will be dealt with."

"I'm just glad it's over," I said.

"Did your parents leave?" José asked me.

"Not yet. They've been spending a lot of time with the Malones."

"Were they close before?"

I shook my head. "They knew each other, but I don't think they'd been in contact for a long time."

"I don't even want to know what they're talking about," Jett said.

I grabbed some popcorn from the microwave. "I'm fine with it so long as I'm not there." I opened the bag and dumped it in a bowl and put it on the table.

"I thought by the time I was this old, my parents would stop embarrassing me and treating me like a teenager," Jett said. "Being the sheriff should make them see me as an adult, but they still boss me around. My mom was even sneaking into my house and cleaning it because she thought I wouldn't do it right."

Boyd grinned. "They're going to see you as a kid until you get married and have kids. It's just the way it is."

"How do you know?" José said. "You didn't get married or have kids."

Boyd laughed. "That's how I know. My parents were still bossing me around when I was fifty."

Creepers came tearing across the kitchen, and Conan followed him. Creepers stopped in front of me and meowed.

"What's wrong?" I asked. He turned and left the room.

"I better follow," I said, walking into the sitting room. He meowed at me again, and I noticed his scratching board had chew marks. "Did the puppy get your things?"

Jett came out carrying Conan. "What's going on?"

"I think Conan chewed up Creepers's scratching board, so he's tattling."

"Did you do that?" Jett asked the puppy, rubbing behind his little ears. Conan barked and wiggled around until Jett put him down.

I smiled. Jett liked Conan more than he was going to admit. I'd caught him baby talking to him this morning when he thought I couldn't hear him.

"Did he sleep any better last night?" I asked.

"A little. I got him to sleep on the bed and not my face, so that's progress."

"Sorry. I feel guilty."

"Don't. Puppies are hard, but I already like the little stinker. Did you teach Zumba today?"

"I was planning on it, but I didn't get the word out fast enough. Barbra and Opal were the only ones who came, and we ended up talking the entire time. They wanted to hear all about the show, so we just sat there. Did you know Barbra's attic is full of stuff from the previous owners?"

"No, but I'm not surprised. I don't see Barbra cleaning her own junk, let alone someone else's."

I smiled. "Just think of the things that might be in there."

Jett groaned. "Let me guess. You've convinced Barbra to let you go through it all?"

"She said maybe."

"Well, if you find a body, just throw a blanket over it and pretend you didn't see it."

I laughed. "I seriously doubt there's a body in Barbra's attic."

"With our luck, there might be."

"The stuff has to be really old."

"So a skeleton?"

"There isn't going to be a skeleton. It might have some things Barbra can sell. Antiques or something fun like that."

"It sounds like a lot of work. You still aren't finished with Barbra's house, are you?"

I shook my head. "No, but I'm getting faster. At first, I took too much time thinking about whether we should throw things out or not. Now I just throw it out unless it jumps out as something worth money or sentimental."

"I thought Barbra thought all her stuff was sentimental?"

I grinned. "She does. She doesn't know what she has, though, so if she doesn't see me throw it out, she doesn't care. In the summer, we're going to have a huge sale and hopefully give her some fun money."

"What are you two doing in here?" Boyd asked as he and José joined us in the living room.

"Just talking," Jett said. "Ivy wants to clean out Barbra's attic."

Boyd chuckled. "Sounds messy."

"I hope you don't find a body," José teased.

"Ha-ha," I said.

Jett sat on the recliner. "That's what I was just saying."

I grabbed Creepers and sat on the armrest of Jett's chair so Boyd and José could sit on the couch.

"I'm not looking for a mystery. Well, maybe a mystery of who the people who lived there were. Don't you all think that would be interesting?"

"Nope," Boyd said. "I'm old. I probably knew the people who lived there. It's not a mystery to me."

"Well, I think it will be fun. If any of you want to join me, you are welcome to—if Barbra lets me. I'm pretty sure I can convince her."

"How long are your parents staying?" José asked me.

"I'm not sure. I can't believe they came without calling. I would have missed them if we'd still been on the train for as long as we were supposed to be. I bet they'll stay a couple of days. My dad isn't retired yet, so he doesn't usually get many vacation days."

"I was talking to both of your moms last night in the diner," Boyd said. "I've known them both since they were born, but I kept confusing their names. Carol, Candy. They aren't that similar, but I must be getting old. Then Carrie came out, and I just stopped using names."

I smiled. "I can see that getting confusing." Creepers jumped off my lap and rubbed against Conan. He must have forgiven him for destroying his things. Conan licked Creepers's head and barked.

"Is there a way to train a dog not to bark? It's probably not good to have a barking dog above the diner."

"Sure," Boyd said. "I'll work on that once he's fully potty trained. One thing at a time is probably best."

"We should do something," Jett said. "Tomorrow, I'm back on duty."

"UNO?" Boyd asked.

"No!" the rest of us all said.

"I was thinking of taking Conan for a walk anyway," Boyd said, picking up the dog.

José stood. "I should go back to the diner. I told Anton he could leave once the morning shift was over. I think he has a date with Livy. I don't want to leave Carrie by herself down there."

Boyd and José left, and I didn't realize I was smiling at the door.

"What is it?" Jett asked.

"I just keep thinking José and Carrie will fall in love eventually, so it's nice when they are the only two in the kitchen."

Jett chuckled. "José and Carrie? I would never have put them together, but now that I think about it, it could work."

"I think she likes him, but she's never straight out said it."

"Do you think he likes her?"

"I can't tell. He does some things that make me wonder. I teased him once, and he left the room, so I haven't done it again."

"I'm going to start watching."

"Don't be obvious about it, or you might scare them."

Jett pulled me onto his lap. "José deserves to be teased. You should have heard the way he teased me before we started dating. That guy was relentless. Only Boyd was worse."

"They both teased me plenty," I said, resting against him. "So what do you want to do? We could go get Barbra to let us in her attic."

"Nah. Let's just sit here and watch a movie. Sometimes being lazy is nice."

"Alright. What do you want to watch?"

"It doesn't matter. I'll probably just end up kissing you the whole time anyway."

I raised my eyebrow. "Oh yeah?"

"Yep. You might want to lock the door. Our parents don't seem to be the type to knock. And why does Boyd have a key?"

I walked over and flipped the lock. "So he can play with my cat. He usually knocks before he comes in, though."

"Our parents should take lessons from him."

"I'm going to get the popcorn," I said, hurrying into the kitchen. "Remind me to make you peanut butter bars sometime. I have a great recipe. I try not to use peanuts at the diner much because so many people have allergies." I brought the popcorn and put it on the end table that used to have my plant Fiona smashed. "I should make Fiona get me a new plant."

"That plant was sad."

"But it might have gotten better."

"I don't think we should talk to Fiona ever again."

I smiled. "I agree. I don't want her admiring your jeans."

"I bet she stays far away from Muddy Creek. She embarrassed herself plenty. I do look good in my jeans, though. You have to admit it."

I grabbed the remote and sat back with Jett. "You do, but you don't have to get a big head about it. Now, should we watch a movie or go clean out Barbra's attic?"

"Definitely a movie," he said, pulling me close and kissing my cheek. "Leave the mysteries for another day."

Peanut Butter Oat Bars with Chocolate Glaze

For the Bars:

- 3/4 cup butter, softened

- 3/4 cup creamy peanut butter

- 3/4 cup granulated sugar

- 3/4 cup packed brown sugar

- 2 large eggs

- 2 teaspoons water

- 1 1/2 teaspoons vanilla extract

- 1 1/2 cups all-purpose flour

- 1 1/2 cups quick-cooking oats

- 3/4 teaspoon baking soda

- 1/2 teaspoon salt

For the Glaze:

- 1 1/2 cups milk chocolate chips

- 1/2 cup creamy peanut butter

Directions

1. Preheat the oven to 325°F. Grease a **15x10x1-inch** baking pan.

2. In a large bowl, beat the butter, peanut butter, granulated sugar, and brown sugar until light and fluffy, about 4 minutes.

3. Add the eggs, water, and vanilla extract, mixing until fully incorporated.

4. In a separate bowl, whisk together the flour, oats, baking soda, and salt. Gradually add this dry mixture to the wet ingredients, mixing until well combined.

5. Spread the batter evenly into the prepared baking pan. Bake for **18-22 minutes**, or until lightly browned.

6. While the bars are baking, prepare the glaze: In a microwave-safe bowl, melt the chocolate chips and peanut butter in 20-second intervals, stirring after each, until smooth.

7. Once the bars are done, pour the glaze over the warm bars, spreading evenly.

8. Allow to cool completely on a wire rack before cutting into squares.

Enjoy!

Also By Kristy Dixon

<u>Cozy Mystery</u>
Murder With a Side of Bacon
Murder With a Hint of Cinnamon
Murder With a Fudge Brownie to Go
Murder With a Splash of Vanilla
Murder With a Drizzle of Syrup

<u>Young Adult</u>
Akkron (The Silver Eclipse Book 1)
Boztoll (The Silver Eclipse Book 2)
The Other Continent (The Silver Eclipse Book 3)

The Amethyst Crown
More Than Once Upon a Time
Trapped In Once Upon a Time
The Beginning of Once Upon a Time
Blade of the Phoenix (Riviand Lost Book 1)
Mermaid's Demise (Riviand Lost Book 2)
Dragon's Cove (Riviand Lost Book 3)
Fairy Lie's (Riviand Lost Book 4)

<u>Coming Soon!</u>
Murder With a Swirl of Blueberry
Forgotten in Once Upon a Time
Rise of the Serpent (Riviand Lost Book 5)

About the Author

Kristy Dixon started writing stories when she was seven and never stopped. She enjoys writing cozy mysteries and YA. At home, she spends her time playing board games with her husband and kids and writing. Occasionally she takes part in a Super Mario marathon. She has six chickens and a cat that help keep life amusing. If she isn't playing with her kids or writing, she is usually eating cookies, or wishing she was eating cookies.

www.ingramcontent.com/pod-product-compliance
Lightning Source LLC
Chambersburg PA
CBHW031042310726
48969CB00007B/2084